TABLE OF CONTENTS

D1716327

P6-BNM-953

Prologue

LOS ANGELES

Sam Tatum was found flat on his back in a parking garage three blocks from the Glendale Galleria at three o'clock on a Wednesday afternoon. Had it started raining an hour later he would have parked on the street and died in a puddle, his face wet with drizzle and his eyes staring up, unblinking, as rain flushed the life from them. The garage had been fate's one courtesy, saving him the embarrassment of dying even more publicly than he did, insofar as corpses can be embarrassed. It was an ignominious death: while he'd expected to die from one too many lines of cocaine up his old man's nose, or murdered, even, in a fit of pique by one of the hustlers he'd been too fond of for too many years, ending his life on the concrete floor of a parking garage, his head in an oil stain, was too seedy even for Sam. Had he been able to think once he was dead, he would have found it a tawdry end to a tawdry life and been glad it was over.

The witnesses assumed it was cardiac arrest. The woman who found him, walking with her 12-year old daughter to their newly purchased Prius parked three cars to the left of Sam's Camry, had worked as a nurse before marrying well and was familiar enough with dead bodies to make the call. The poor guy was old, out of shape, uncommonly pale, and obviously lived an unhealthy life. He was lucky to make it this far, she thought, more disturbed that her child had seen a corpse than that he was actually dead. She didn't know him, what was it to her? Mostly it was an inconvenience, since she had the decency to call an ambulance, knowing it was much too late to save the poor slob, and stay around to speak to the police. She'd considered making it an anonymous 911 call, since her daughter's ballet class started at 3:30 and this would mean missing it for sure. But something in her, that old nurse calling, that instinct to do the right thing, made her give her name and location and wait patiently for the paramedics who would try to resuscitate a man she knew was dead. His eyes were open, for godsake, and what life had been in them had slipped away some time ago. Anyone could see that.

She'd told her daughter Kelly to get into the car the moment she saw the man's feet come into view. Kelly, being a precocious, ballet-class-taking 12-year-old, wanted the full view and instead of doing what she was told rushed around ahead of her mother to get a good look. She had never seen a dead body before and she could tell by her mother's lack of urgency that the man was probably beyond help. After an inappropriate but predictable, "Cool!", she obeyed her mother and skipped ahead to their car. Once inside, she tweeted that she and her mother had found a dead guy, and waited for her friends' texts to start flooding in.

Sam's death was twelfth-page news, not more than a brief item for the curious, a paragraph about a man found dead near the Glendale Galleria. The reporter for the Glendale News-Press gave it a quick once-over, not bothering to call the coroner's office or find out any significant details about Sam Tatum's life and death. News had to flow constantly these days, and most of that was from wire services and Google alerts. Real reporting was a dying profession, and the News-Press hack was happy not to expend too much energy on dead old fat men in parking garages. If the death wasn't important enough to make the L.A. Times, why the hell should he bother with it? So it ran as a sidebar, a snippet, given about as much notice as Sam Tatum had been given most of his life.

There was one website, however, that specialized in unusual deaths, which Sam's turned out to be. *DeathWatchLA.com* had begun in the 1970s as a sort of gossip rag for the morbidly obsessed. Back then it was just a couple pages offering lurid details of murders both sensational and obscure, so long as they were noteworthy for their gruesomeness or peculiarity. An accidental decapitation could sell an extra thousand copies. Run of the mill heart attacks didn't make the grade; as it turned out, Sam Tatum's death was not run of the mill.

With the arrival of the internet the creepy little paper became a big attractive website, and even though its founder had died in a way befitting a banner headline – found stuffed in the trunk of a Lincoln town car – his sons knew a gold mine when they had one and turned the site into a million-hits-a-month bonanza. They expanded with sister sites (*DeathWatchNYC*, *DeathWatchCHI*, even a *DeathWatchMinneapolis*), death tours, both walking and by hearse, and planned to launch their own malt liquor in a few months. Meanwhile, they had content to keep up and readers to satisfy, and as much as one might not expect it, there were fans of the ordinary who found a parking lot death-by-ice pick as fascinating as a decomposed celebrity. For that is how Sam Tatum had really died: an ice pick (as close as the coroner could guess on a murder weapon) slipped quickly, almost expertly, into the base of his skull, shoved at an upward angle to ensure instant death and very little blood loss. It seems someone had wanted Sam dead and had found the perfect opportunity – the third floor of a parking garage with no more than a dozen cars parked in it and no witnesses. How they came upon him was anyone's guess. There appeared to be no signs of conflict, not even a sign of alarm. Had it been someone he knew? Or simply someone he felt unthreatened by? No one would ever know, but *DeathWatchLA* certainly posed the questions.

Thus it was that someone on the other side of the country who happened to read *DeathWatchLA* took notice and knew that the email he'd gotten from Sam two weeks earlier was not the panic of a man who had used too many drugs and bought too many young men. Sam Tatum was dead. He had not been paranoid, but convinced someone was after them, and he had been right. Three months earlier there had been another death, a man named Frank Grandy, this one in Detroit. Neither of them had spoken to

Frank in years, and it was only when Frank had left Sam $2000 in his will as a very belated repayment of a loan, that Sam knew their old partner in crime was dead. No suspects had been named, no one identified, but the report mentioned an antique pocket watch Frank was selling on an internet auction site. The watch case was there, but the watch was gone. Robbery, they assumed, but the investigation had gone nowhere. That was what rang the alarm bell for Sam, the watch. He was surprised Frank had kept it all these years, but not surprised it had led to his death. The past, it seems, had been waiting patiently to find them, and it had.

The two deaths spoke not of coincidence, but of a plan, with a planner and only one target left. The *DeathWatchLA* reader logged off his computer, swiveled around in his desk chair and cheerfully took a cup of coffee from his partner, smiling as if nothing had changed and they were simply beginning another gorgeous day. Time to get started.

Chapter One

PRIDE LODGE

Halloween weekend was the busiest of the year at Pride Lodge, with the Fourth of July a close second. Gay people like a party, and the Halloween parties at the Lodge had been legendary for twenty-five years. Rooms in the main lodge and the six adjoining cabins were sold out by mid-summer, all in anticipation of a fiendishly good time in the Pennsylvania countryside not quite like anything the guests would find elsewhere. It was city meets country in a unique and intimate setting far from the streets of New York or Philadelphia. Everybody knew everybody here, and among the delights for guests was seeing friends they hadn't hugged or shared a drink with since last Halloween.

Pride Lodge sits on ten acres along Pennsylvania's Highway 32, just 20 minutes from New Hope and a short walk to the Delaware River. Originally an old farmhouse, the Lodge had been converted into an inn in the early 1950s. Bed and breakfasts weren't all the rage then, and the idea of having an inn along a country road, surrounded by woods and farmland and catering to people who wanted something out of their way, was a novelty. So much of a novelty that the business failed and the original owners, well-intended but bankrupt, sold it to new owners, who sold it to newer owners. Finally, in the mid-1980s, the inn was dilapidated, its windows boarded up for longer than

1

anyone could remember, and the last owner was selling the land. That was when Pucky Green and Stu Patterson, partners in life and whatever business venture they'd cooked up at the time, decided it was a perfect place for a gay resort. It proved to be the one stroke of genius and the one true success they ever had, aside from deciding to spend their lives together.

They renovated the old inn and re-christened it Pride Lodge. They added on to the main two-story building until it had eight guest rooms on the first floor and six on the second, along with what they called the Master Suite, where the two of them lived. The Lodge boasted a functioning restaurant and bar adjoining the main room, which everyone call the "great room", complete with fireplace, wide-screen television, three mahogany book shelves to give the space a library feel, and a check-in desk where you could buy the usual rainbow paraphernalia, along with a Pride Lodge sweatshirt and baseball cap, should you be in the market for souvenirs. Three years into the venture, when they realized it was going to succeed, they added a swimming pool, and two years after that they had six cabins built, each with two spacious "luxury" rooms that included kitchenettes and private baths. They had the inn's cavernous basement sound-proofed and converted half into a piano bar called Clyde's and half into a karaoke room. The combined entertainment had the effect of bringing in locals for dinner and a night out, helping to swell the numbers without having to add more rooms. The whole undertaking took five years, but once it was completed it was a sight to behold: a resort for gays, lesbians, bisexuals, and more than a few transgender visitors, well before the term had been officially coined. Back then everyone just called it a gay resort, with the knowledge that all were welcome, including the occasional, befuddled heterosexual couple who pulled into the driveway because they liked the name of the place. Most of them politely drove on once they got to the desk and realized there was something different going on here. Maybe it was the two slightly masculine women sitting by the fireplace, or the restaurant hostess with the Adam's apple, but now and then they stayed and were made to feel as much at home as any other guest.

Pucky was the ringmaster, the chatty, gregarious captain of this strange and colorful ship. A diminutive man at five-five, he had a habit of keeping his hair dyed strawberry blond and wearing a collection of eyeglasses to rival a young Elton John's. Pucky loved his glasses, all of them prescription and required for him to see three feet beyond his nose, and he would wear a different pair each week, starting over every six weeks for the six pairs he owned. He wore Hawaiian shirts in the summer and high-end casual short-sleeved shirts the rest of the year, always with long pants. Pucky didn't like his legs; he thought they were too chickeny, as he called them, and he never exposed them in public, which meant he never used the swimming pool. He was the face of Pride Lodge, the official greeter, taskmaster of a ragtag staff, and the table floater at dinner who went from guest to guest asking how their food was, if their rooms were up to snuff, and if there was anything at all he could help them with, excluding the sexual encounters some of the guests hoped for after an hour or two at the bar. That, Pucky discreetly let them know, was up to them. He was many things, with many hats, but a pimp was not one of them.

Stu had met Pucky when they were both in the United States Navy stationed at the Naval Air Station in Key West. Had it been up to Stu they would still be living there. He much preferred the tropical climate of the Florida Keys, but even more important to him was the man he'd fallen in love with and to whom he'd committed his life way back in 1972. A world away, a time removed, when Vietnam was still unresolved and an American president had yet to resign in disgrace.

Stu was silence to Pucky's noise, calm to Pucky's chaos. He stayed in the background, even though everyone knew who he was. Stu did the Lodge's books and looked after the financial end of things. He liked that. He was a thinker, a lover of novels and quiet. Running Pride Lodge might seem like an odd choice for a man who preferred the company of only one person, but it worked well for Stu. He had life in the country. He had Pucky to look after the guests and keep the occasional madness away from him. And he had a companion for life, his one great treasure. It made aging, going bald, feeling his knees begin to buckle and the weight slowly add to his once tall, slender frame, not quite so discomfiting.

One morning three years ago Stu was taking his dawn constitutional, as he called it, walking around the grounds as the sun was just beginning to rise. He would have a single cup of de-caffeinated coffee in the Suite's kitchen while it was still dark out; then he would put on his coat if the weather was chill, as it had been that September, and he would walk slowly around the cabins, along the periphery of the property and back up past the pool, climbing the stairs that led to the Lodge just as the sun was climbing the morning sky. That was where they found him, on the stairs, almost at the top, as if, had he made it three more steps, he would still be alive. His heart had stopped, outlasted by his knees and every other part of him, as he made his way slowly up the stairs. The one small mercy was that Ricki, the long-time desk manager, night time restaurant hostess and summer pool boy – if you can call a 50-year-old man a boy – was the one who found him. Ricki slept very little, which helped explain how he managed to be so many things to so many people, and it was his habit to drive in from his home in Lambertville, across the river in New Jersey, and clean the bars first thing in the morning. When he parked his car that day he noticed what looked like a red jacket on the steps leading up to the Lodge. At first he assumed someone had had too much to drink the night before and lost their jacket, but then he noticed a pair of beige pants running below the jacket and an arm stuck straight out to the side and he suddenly realized it was a person, lying face down and motionless. He rushed over to find Stu, dead with his glasses cracked on his face from where he'd hit the step, those stupid old black horn-rims Pucky had been on him for years to replace. He rolled Stu over and, not knowing the first thing about CPR, tried to save him anyway, stopping in the frantic effort to shout, "Help! Help! Somebody help!"

Pucky tried to carry on without Stu but everyone could tell it wasn't going to work. He stopped greeting people, he stopped paying attention to detail, and within a few months he stopped caring altogether. He decided to sell Pride Lodge and retire to Key West. The one other place he knew Stu loved and would probably have preferred to live, but he had loved Pucky even more. He would sell the Lodge, where his heart had stopped on those steps as surely as Stu's had, and he would go to the southernmost end of the country, buy a small condo, and live out his life with his memories.

Word spread quickly that Pucky was selling. Fear set in among the regulars that the famed and beloved Pride Lodge would end up in the hands of a developer who cared not a whit for its history, and the collective memory of all the friends and guests who had stayed there would quickly fade, blown away as easily and dismissively as ash.

That was when Sid Stanhope and Dylan Tremblay stepped in. Ten years apart in age, with Sid the older at sixty-two that year, they were longtime guests of the Lodge who drove in from their home in Long Branch, New Jersey, several times a year to spend long weekends. Sid was about ready to retire from his job as an assistant bank manager, having hoped the past five years not to be laid off; he saw this as a golden opportunity to get out before he was pushed out, despite the tragic circumstances that had the Lodge on the market. Dylan had never been content to begin with, job hopping his entire adult life until he found his job of the last six years selling men's clothes in a store whose only claim to fame was having survived in Long Branch. The boardwalk there had been built up over the last decade, with high-end condos along the shore. Life in Long Branch wasn't quite the depressing reality it had been, but the chance to get out? To buy Pride Lodge and live out their lives there, as Pucky and Stu had? It was just the sort of stroke of luck, that accident of timing, you could wait most of your life for. When it happened you had to act. Sid and Dylan acted, and two years later, as they decorated the Lodge for another Halloween, they still thought it was the best move they'd ever made.

Chapter Two

CABIN 6

Kyle Callahan and Danny Durban arrived at Pride Lodge late on Thursday night. This was their fifth Halloween at the Lodge and an event they both looked forward to starting several months before October. The couple had spent three long weekends each year there for the five years they'd been together, one for each season excluding winter. As lovely as the Pennsylvania countryside was, Kyle and Danny both found it too bare, too cold and stark in the winter months.

They'd found Pride Lodge by accident their first summer together, after Kyle suggested they go away for a weekend and began a brief internet search of gay bed and breakfasts within driving distance of their apartment in Manhattan. Pride Lodge popped up, just 90 minutes by rental car. While it was much larger than a traditional B&B, it instantly became one of their favorite getaways, and five years later they'd made the drive again as October came to a close and the Halloween festivities promised friendship, fun and an escape for them both from the pressures of their lives in the City.

Ricki was just about to go off desk duty when they arrived at nearly eleven o'clock that night. He knew all the regular guests well and was delighted to see them, even though he'd known they were coming. Several other guests had arrived early as well and a few were having drinks by the fireplace as Kyle and Danny checked in and got the key for Cabin 6. They always stayed in Cabin 6. For one thing, it was one of the luxury rooms, with its own television, kitchenette and bathroom (guests who stayed in the main lodge had to share one of four bathrooms); it was also well away and just down the road, giving the roomers a greater sense of privacy. The cabins were surrounded by trees in back and a long private drive in front. Most of the people who stayed at Pride Lodge were older. It just wasn't the kind of place young LGBT travelers went to for a good time: too remote, too sedate, and too, well, old. The perfect hideaway for mature gay men and lesbian couples and singles looking to be comfortable exposing their 40 or 50 or 60 year old bodies in a bathing suit, or sitting around a restaurant bar chatting with other people who remembered music from the 1970s when it was new and who would not likely be spending their time tweeting, linking in or obsessively checking their smart phones for texts and celebrity news flashes.

The other reason they always stayed in Cabin 6 was the painting: a beautiful dark-haired woman in a flowing red dress sitting at a black grand piano in front of a fireplace. She looked as if she were frozen in the 1940s, and appeared to be posing at the piano more than actually playing it. There was sheet music in front of her, but only one's imagination could decide what the music was. Classical, most certainly, given the elegance of the woman and the room. It was clearly a reproduction, something that must surely be hanging in thousands of homes and hotel rooms around the world, but Kyle had only ever seen it in one other place – above his mother's piano in the home he had grown up in in Highland Park, Illinois. His mother moved to a condo in Chicago after his father's death and she had taken the picture with her. Kyle saw it in her bedroom the two or three times a year he and Danny made their trips to visit. (Sally and Bert Callahan were married for forty-seven years before Bert's death, and Sally had made it very clear that her son would be the only other man in her life for the rest of it. While Kyle thought she was young and vibrant enough to meet someone new, she would hear none of it; he respected it, accepted it, and kept it out of their conversations.)

Kyle had noticed the painting on their first stay at the Lodge. It was by accident and at a most inopportune time: they had checked in and were having sex, something they did with more urgency and frequency in those early days. No sooner had Danny closed the cabin door and turned the lock, than Kyle was slipping his clothes off and nodding toward the bed. Fifty may have been just around the corner for them both, but age had not diminished their desire and only added to their skills at pleasing one another. Their sexual relationship had been one of mutual giving from the first time they'd enjoyed it – after the third or fourth date, depending on which of them you asked. They were post-top/bottom, beyond the old constraints of roles, and more than anything, they simply enjoyed the intimacy they shared. It was, they believed, the real essence of a lasting physical bond: simply being close, touching, caressing, holding one another with a breeze cooling them as it swept in the window.

Twenty minutes later, with Danny lying naked next to him, his head on Kyle's chest, Kyle glanced above his head and saw the painting for the first time. It startled him. It was early in their time together and Kyle, never a superstitious man, took it as some kind of message, as if his parents were giving their blessing in a discreet but very unusual way. Kyle made sure he and Danny stayed in Cabin 6 every visit after that. Pucky, Stu and Ricki all considered it Kyle and Danny's room when they came, but Kyle never told them why and they never asked, and if by some error someone else was booked into Cabin 6 when Kyle called to make a reservation, they were quietly moved. That was the kind of service you could expect at Pride Lodge, and what kept its loyal devotees coming back.

Kyle Callahan met Danny Durban when both men were forty-seven, with just six months separating them. Danny, being the older of the pair, joked that theirs was a May-June romance. They stumbled upon one another, literally, at a photography exhibit at the Katherine Pride Gallery in Chelsea's Meatpacking District. Kyle had gone because of his love for photography and his passion as an amateur photographer. Danny had gone because the owner of the gallery, Katherine Pride, had recently become a customer at Margaret's Passion, the long-time Gramercy Park restaurant where Danny was the day manager. It was the kind of personal touch Margaret's was known for, securing in return a legendary loyalty to the restaurant and to Margaret herself. The only meat to be found in the Meatpacking District these days came on very high-priced plates at restaurants with names like Sacrosanct and Tiberius. The area had once housed butchers feeding the citizens of New York City; now it was all upscale eateries, art galleries and clothing stores. Kyle had come around a corner, studying the photographs on the wall, and accidentally bumped into Danny, spilling both their drinks. Their eyes met an instant before their smiles, and five years later they were discussing the logistics of a wedding – not if, but when for the two men now that they could marry in New York.

Kyle Callahan was by most measures an average looking man. He'd often been mistaken for someone else, with strangers saying to him, "You remind me of someone," then proceeding to be unable to say whom. He had a generic look about him: oval face, large nose he'd inherited from the women (yes, the women) in his family; pale blue eyes that were strikingly un-striking, the sort of blue eyes no one remarked upon or would be able to recall as blue unless they were asked while looking directly at him. His hair had been blond as a child but had long since turned brown, and he kept it cropped close to his skull, in part to downplay a receding hairline. He would never be bald, but the frontline of his forehead seemed to retreat a quarter inch or so every few years. He dressed in slacks and button-down shirts, in and out of the office, not liking the heaviness of blue jeans even on vacation; and his one surrender to fashion was his glasses: progressive, transitional, bifocal Ray-Bans that just about everyone said were the coolest glasses they'd seen.

Danny was the more outgoing of the two. He was also six inches shorter than Kyle, who was not a particularly tall man. It was a height difference Kyle never noticed except when he saw pictures of them together. Danny was the talker, Kyle the brooder. Danny preferred shorts outside his job in all but the coldest weather, and would throw on a sweatshirt or sweater to compensate for a chill, only resorting to blue jeans if it was below 45 degrees or they were going somewhere where shorts would be inappropriate. He liked being as casual as possible outside the restaurant where he had worked for the past ten years. He was top talent, keeping Margaret's customers happy, familiar and returning. Margaret Bowman was a real person, and running a restaurant had been the only thing she'd ever wanted to succeed at since watching her parents run an Italian eatery for thirty years. She was a cheerful, birdlike woman, thin and always in a dress, who seldom came down to the restaurant anymore from her apartment above it on East 21st Street, but when she did she always caused a stir. Margaret was a neighborhood fixture and a shrewd businesswoman who knew from watching her mother all those years it was the personal touch that mattered. She would go slowly from table to table saying hello to people who had known and loved her for years. She asked how their children and grandchildren were; if there was a young couple dining she would remark on how lovely they looked together. If they were single, divorced, or even grieving the loss of a loved one, Margaret somehow knew and would say exactly the right thing. She had lost her husband Gerard to cancer some years back and had no children, and she considered Danny the son she had always wanted. She would not have hesitated, however, to let him go had he not been the very best at his job. She was as demanding as she was loyal, and Danny hoped the years would slow just a little not only for himself but to keep Margaret around as long as possible.

Kyle was the personal assistant to Imogene Landis, a high-maintenance, high-octane, high-profile television reporter whose star had been falling steadily for the past five years, which is exactly how long Kyle had worked for her. It seems she had found the best assistant she'd ever had – or at least the most persevering – just as her career began its slow slide into the tank of obscurity. Before Kyle, no one had lasted more than a year working for Imogene, and for that determination and loyalty she repaid him by being as needy, intrusive and inappropriate as she possibly could.

The only thing small about Imogene was her height: the tiny woman had a mouth three times her size with a fondness for profanity. She stood a mere five feet tall in heels and had never weighed more than a hundred pounds; her hair had gone through several styles over the years, settling most recently on a sort of refurbished, resurrected bob ("Horrible," Danny said when he saw the new style. "Absolutely awful, but you told her you loved it, I know you did.") Imogene had changed jobs nearly as often as she'd changed assistants. She complained to Kyle that it was ageism, that an almost-star TV reporter-personality in her late 40s was simply not a product anyone was selling, with the emphasis on selling: there was a demographic hungry for her, she insisted, a demographic just like her who were tired of a youth culture that erased them as quickly as it could, the buyers for whom Imogene's bosses had nothing to offer. That would change, she knew it would, as America's hairs all turned gray with just a little touchup, and she would be there ready to step into the part. Kyle thought her employment problems had more to do with her habit of telling her superiors what she really thought of them, even, most recently, when it was disgust at her producer's marital indiscretions with an intern. The man didn't take too well to that and, once more, Imogene saw a staff announcement telling her and everyone else that she would be looking for new adventures and was wished well by all. Kyle suspected her current job, as a special English-language correspondent on financial affairs for Tokyo Pulse, a third-tier Japanese cable show produced by Japan TV3, was the last stop on this train. She'd be editing copy or selling Avon if she blew this one. He thought she knew it, too, which was why she leaned on him more than ever and why he allowed it. He confessed to a kind of love for Imogene, a soft spot for a woman whose vulnerabilities she would never admit to herself, and he planned to see the job through to whatever end it met.

"Please turn your phone off," Danny said as they rolled their luggage into Cabin 6. He knew the third person on every vacation they took was Imogene Landis and he wanted her left in Manhattan; that included limiting her digital reach, ignoring her texts and letting her go to voicemail.

"Just let me check the emails, then I'll turn it off for the night. I promise."

"For the night? We're not just here for the night. I'm telling you, it's not a coincidence you met us both at the same time. The universe was determined I couldn't have you to myself."

"Right. As if Margaret and her restaurant aren't your first love. I know very well what it's like to have to share."

"She's eighty years old, for godsake, well, as of next Wednesday. Imogene is going to last a looooot longer. Think about that before you answer her next cry for help."

"She's at the Stock Exchange tomorrow morning, it's a very big deal for her."

"In the background! She's a prop, Kyle, she's not ringing the bell."

"Be kind. The show airs in Tokyo."

"A re-run at 3:00 am. On cable, with Japanese sub-titles. She doesn't speak a word of the language."

"Of course not, that's why they hired her! She's an English-language correspondent. Do I need to explain what that is?"

Danny glared at Kyle. The two men were as made for each other as a couple could be, but like any couple they each had habits and attitudes the other had grudgingly learned to deal with. One of Kyle's was his condescension, and while Danny knew it wasn't meant to be insulting, he didn't like it. "I know what an English-language correspondent is," he said slowly, causing Kyle to blush. "I know what a good one is, too."

Kyle started to protest in defense of his boss, but Danny cut him off with a wave of his hand. "It's great she's learning Japanese, it really is," Danny said. "She'll be able to tell her bosses to fuck off in their own language, maybe do a proper bow with it."

"She's learned her lesson."

"Several times."

Danny saw the hurt on Kyle's face. "I'm sorry. I know you're devoted to her, but she's not the one you're marrying. And she'll get over the trauma of standing three people to the side, back row I'm sure, at the opening bell of the Stock Exchange. She can be your best man . . . or best woman or however it's done with gay people."

The two men had been talking about marriage since the law passed in New York. They'd been cautious, not wanting to get caught up in the emotions of the moment. They decided against rushing down to City Hall as they thought many couples had without really thinking it through. But they were in negotiations, so to speak. Marriage, once it became a reality, was a serious step, and Kyle and Danny would take it in their own time, as wisely as two men who knew they'd spend the rest of their lives together could.

Danny began hanging his shirts in the closet and putting his underwear, socks and sundries in the top dresser drawer.

Kyle rolled his suitcase into a corner by the nightstand on his side of the bed. He tended to vacation out of his suitcase and was never in a hurry to unpack. This was not their apartment, and he figured the task of hanging up shirts and pants could wait until morning. His real concern was his camera. He'd upgraded to a Nikon D3100. At $600 it wasn't all that top of the line, but it was the best he'd ever had and he was extremely protective of it, treating it the way a violinist might treat a Stradivarius. He had been in love with photography since his father gave him a new camera for his fortieth birthday. Late in life to find a passion, but never too late. He discovered to his surprise that he had a good eye for framing pictures, and a unique sensibility. He had started a photoblog, AsKyleSeesIt, on Tumblr last year, and very quickly had a following. Mostly other amateur shutterbugs, but now and then he would get a comment from a pro who told him he should be selling his work. He didn't consider himself a blogger, really, not a man to offer opinions. He was just a guy who liked taking pictures and now he could share them online. He walked around with his camera always slung over his neck, bouncing against his chest. He was always looking for that good photo, that surprising image. He was especially intrigued with angles: he would look up at ceilings, or turn his head sideways in a train station, always wondering how what he saw would translate onto a digital picture. And he took them, lots of them. He also specialized in capturing people who didn't know they were being photographed. He would let the camera hang around his neck with his right hand resting lazily on it, as if keeping it from swinging back and forth. When he saw someone he wanted to snap, he would glance away from them, his version of the magician's art of misdirection, click the shutter button, and hope for the best. It had taken a while to master: he initially cut off people's heads, or he would get a picture of their legs, or end up with someone so unfocused you couldn't tell it was a person. But eventually he got it down, and now he could stroll along any street in Manhattan, or walk through any mall in any town, and if he saw someone interesting, they were his; it was magic, capturing completely un-guarded, unpracticed expressions, humanity as it really looks when it thinks no one is watching.

Kyle checked his camera to make sure he had the battery charger and the USB cable to upload photos to his laptop. He'd checked at home before they left, of course, but these were the sorts of small details people tended to run through their minds over and over: Did I turn the stove off, did I lock the door? Once he confirmed he had not forgotten anything, he sat on the edge of the bed and took out his phone. It was a smart phone, they all were these days (as opposed to a dumb phone, he wondered?). That's why he owned it – to read emails, texts, use applications, search the internet, and upload the occasional photograph to his blog. He seldom used it as a telephone, and he wondered how long it would be before the word "phone" was dropped altogether from the devices. The only three people he spoke to with it were Imogene (mostly), Danny (when he wasn't at a landline), and his mother in Chicago. He sometimes called her from his home phone, which was also his desk phone. Kyle had a cubicle at Japan TV3 next to Imogene's (she had not had an office since two jobs back) but preferred to work at home when he could, given Imogene's frequent absences from the station as she interviewed financial subordinates and C-list economists happy just to get a microphone in front of them.

He scrolled through his emails and saw that Danny was right, as he knew he would be. Seven emails from Imogene, all stealth with subject lines like, "HAVE A GREAT TIME!" and "TAKE LOTS OF PIX FOR ME!" She had never accepted that all-caps was bad form. And below the screaming demands that he enjoy himself she would type something frantic, urgent, or personal-time-interrupting. Kyle had been onto this trick for years but she still thought he fell for it.

He decided to keep his promise to Danny and leave Imogene's emails until the morning, when he could respond to them calmly, reassuring her that the earth had not shifted beneath her feet the past twenty-four hours. He was just about to turn off his phone when he saw the alert for a text message. Odd, he thought, looking at the time stamp. It had come in at 10:00 p.m. but they'd been pulling into the Lodge right about then. He hadn't heard any alert, and he never had his phone on vibrate. The text was from Teddy Pembroke, Pride Lodge's jack-of-all-trades. Teddy had been with the Lodge for fifteen years and was the only person other than Sid and Dylan who lived on the property.

The text read: "Let me know when u arrive. Things have gone wrong. Acceptance."

"Hmm," Kyle said, staring at the message, then looking at the night-stand. 11:30 p.m.

"What?" asked Danny, zipping up his now-empty suitcase and sliding it under the bed.

"Teddy texted me." He showed Danny the message. "Is it too late to call?"

"Yes," Danny said, glancing at the clock. "And what's with the 'acceptance'?"

"It's a quote, from the book they use in Alcoholics Anonymous. Kind of a mantra for him. I should call."

"It can wait." Danny smiled and held up a small bottle of massage oil he'd brought with him.

The two men had spent a weekend the previous spring at a retreat billed as "an erotic getaway" for couples and singles who wanted to explore what the facilitator Don called their "sensual selves." Their sex life at the five-year mark was still vigorous, but not nearly as crucial as it had once seemed. It was about the quality, not the quantity, and while both of them accepted that this was the course nearly every relationship took as it withstood the test of time, there were ways to spice it up and keep it interesting. Much of the time at the retreat had been spent naked, with partners exploring each other's bodies, and, in some cases, but not Kyle and Danny's, the bodies of the other weekenders. Danny held a poor view of open relationships, and while Kyle wasn't judgmental about it, he had always known it was not for him. Monogamy came with the territory for both of them, and when Danny had suggested the workshop, Kyle thought it might be just what they needed. One result was the massages they enjoyed, taking turns being the masseur. Tonight was Danny's turn.

Kyle smiled at Danny, trying to hide his unease about the text message. He'd befriended Teddy on their first visit to the Lodge and had kept in touch with him through the occasional email and a phone call now and then. Teddy had called him two days earlier to make sure they were still coming.

"It's Halloween," Kyle told him. "We never miss Halloween."

"Good," Teddy had said. He sounded nervous on the call, edgy. "I won't be staying at the Lodge much longer, Kyle. Something's going on, we need to talk."

"What, Teddy? Just tell me."

"Not on the phone. I'm not even sure if I'm imagining some of this, it's confusing, but somebody needs to know. You're good at helping me sort things out, Kyle, it can wait two days."

Kyle had become Teddy's reluctant confidant, especially the last year. Teddy was close to Kyle's age but had never done much more than handyman work and odd jobs. Clearly once handsome, with chocolate brown eyes that were as seductive as they were sad, a mouth that had a habit of biting its upper lip, and still thin when most men his age were packing on weight, Teddy seemed as if he were from the coulda-been-a-contender school. Had he gotten more education, had he applied himself more intently, and especially had he not been an alcoholic. That was where Kyle had helped him most, connecting him with a local man Kyle knew was in Alcoholics Anonymous. Kyle wasn't in AA and had never had a drinking problem, but he was very good at finding sources and researching – it's part of what he does for a living – and after a few failed starts, Teddy had finally gotten sober six months ago. Maybe, Kyle thought, that's what this was about. Maybe Teddy had concluded he could no longer work at the Lodge and needed to move on for the sake of his sobriety. He had already stopped helping Cowboy Dave and Happy in the bar. That's when it occurred to him this might be about love.

"Is there something wrong with you and Happy?" Kyle asked. He knew Teddy and the much younger Happy Corcoran, who had started as a bar back the summer before, had been dating. Young man breaks old man's heart, Kyle thought to himself, old man folds up his tent and runs away.

There was a moment of silence on the other end. Then Teddy said, his voice lowered as if someone might hear him, "Happy's gone. Since yesterday, without a word. I'm afraid it's my fault."

"He's a kid," Kyle said, immediately regretting it. Happy was twenty-five or thereabouts and capable of making adult decisions. "A broken heart at that age . . ."

"That's not what I mean," Teddy said. "I told him things I shouldn't have told him, and now he's gone."

"What, Teddy?" Kyle said, his exasperation showing. "What did you tell him?"

"Not on the phone." And then, with a sadness Kyle could feel from 70 miles away, "He wouldn't just leave me."

The call ended then, with Teddy not wanting to say anymore until they spoke in person. Whatever the problem was, it had Teddy itchy, sounding paranoid, and the sudden disappearance of Happy could only make it worse.

"You're sure it's too late?" Kyle asked, looking at the clock again.

"Let them man sleep," Danny said, and Kyle could hear the top of the massage oil bottle flip open. "You'll see him at breakfast."

Kyle decided Danny was right. Teddy worked long hours, pretty much from sun up till helping close down the restaurant at 9:30 each night. He didn't need Kyle waking him up over a text message.

Kyle turned his phone off, waiting to make sure it actually shut down (it had a strange habit of coming back to life, as if it didn't appreciate being told what to do). He set it on the nightstand, then stood up and started to unbutton his shirt.

"I can do that," Danny said, motioning Kyle onto the bed. "I haven't forgotten how."

Kyle let it all go then, enjoying the touch of the man he was already growing old with. He picked up the bottle of almond oil and poured some onto this hand, then began to slide it over his chest. "Let me help you," he said, smiling at Danny as his shirt fell to the floor. Teddy was probably asleep by now, and Kyle was quickly forgetting what the fuss had been all about.

Chapter Three

ROOM 202

S he liked the idea of being a lesbian assassin and wondered if there were others like her, how they would go about finding one other, if they did. Maybe there was some sort of Facebook page for her kind, some site that required coded phrases and passwords to enter, but once inside she would not be alone in her singular mission, her only drive. It had been very lonely, and while she allowed her imagination its moments, she knew she did not belong in the company of killers. She'd had no choice in the matter, and was not really an assassin. Assassins were sent by others, were they not? They did the bidding of paymasters, while the assassin herself might have no stake in the matter at all. It was just a job, a high-risk paycheck. There was no comparison to be made. Hers was a mission of justice, of setting right a world that had been tilted wickedly out of balance thirty years ago when she was just a ten year old child hiding in a closet.

She had heard the men break into their home in Los Feliz, an affluent section of Los Angeles with its own boulevard snaking along past the Greek Theatre, east toward Glendale. She and her parents were supposed to be on a flight to London, part vacation, part present for her tenth birthday, but she had fallen seriously ill with a flu (there it was again, the guilt; it had been her fault somehow, another reason she must make amends and end these lives) and they had postponed the trip. Had they gone, had she not complained or registered a fever, her parents would be alive and her life would have had a completely different trajectory than the one leading her here, to this strange lodge outside a town she'd never been to or planned to see again.

Her childhood bedroom was on the second floor down the hall from her parents' room. She hadn't been able to sleep, tossing and turning, sweating with her fever, and when she heard the glass shatter she thought at first she had imagined or dreamt it. That's what fevers do to you. She sat up in bed and listened, hearing what to her was the distinct sound of someone in the house. She hurried out of bed in her nightgown and tip-toed quickly down the hall. Her father had always been a heavy sleeper, and her mother had the habit of using ear plugs to soften the sound of her husband's snores. Emily — that was her name then — went to her father and shook him awake.

"Daddy! Daddy!" she said, rocking him furiously. "There's somebody downstairs!"

Carl Lapinsky pulled himself from a deep sleep as quickly as he could, like a man swimming furiously up toward the surface. The alarm in his daughter's voice told him there was no time to waste, and he put his fingers to his lips to tell her to be silent: he'd heard her perfectly well, even blanketed by sleep, and he leaned up on one elbow to listen to the silence outside the room.

There it was, the sound of hushed voices. Carl cursed himself for not turning on the alarm. He'd seen a news report just the other day about the folly of having an alarm system you didn't turn on when you were home. Men especially thought they didn't need an alarm to protect a house they were in. It didn't occur to them that the alarm was there to protect them and their families, not their possessions. Now, in the darkness with the sound of intruders coming up the stairs, Carl knew he would never make that mistake again.

His wife Barbara had woken up, disturbed by the commotion in her bed, and was taking out her earplugs when Carl told his daughter to get into the closet and stay there. She did as her father told her, rushing to the closet and hunching down below her mother's dresses, leaving the door open just a crack.

It was Carl Lapinsky's second mistake, and a fatal one. He owned a gun, but kept it in the closet, where he had just sent his daughter to hide. He cursed himself for not thinking clearly, and wondered if he had time to rush to the closet and get the gun he kept in a box on the shelf. He would try, he had to. He made a gesture of fingers-to-lips, shhhh, to his wife, and swung his legs off the bed, about to dash to the closet when a man stepped into the doorway.

"What the fuck?" the man said. Clearly he had been surprised to find them there.

Carl turned and saw him: a squat man, thick with a barrel chest, but an intelligent face that registered, in that instant, curiosity as much as menace. Even in the darkness Carl could make out the man's appearance. He was wearing a blue or green flannel shirt, gray windbreaker, blue jeans, white sneakers and a belt with a ridiculously large silver buckle on it. One of those country-western type buckles you'd expect to find at a roadside honky-tonk holding up some fake cowboy's pants. It did not belong with the sneakers and windbreaker, and Carl was wondering why anyone would wear a belt buckle like that without boots when the man slid a gun from his jacket pocket and shot Carl in the head. Barbara was fully awake by then, staring at the scene as if she were still dreaming. She screamed for only a moment before the man shot her, too. Two people dead, just like that. Two people who weren't supposed to be there.

From inside the closet Emily heard sounds of footsteps rushing into the bedroom. More men, though she couldn't tell how many.

"What the fuck are you doing?" shrieked one man.

"They startled me," said the shooter. "What was I supposed to do?"

"Not kill them," said a third. "We don't kill people. We don't even carry guns. Why are you bringing a gun?"

"You're a moron," said the shooter. "We break into homes. Did it never occur to you that just such a thing might happen? And that we'd be the ones staring at the barrel of a shotgun? That's why I carry a gun, asshole."

"You're the asshole."

"No, you're the asshole. I just saved our lives!"

"By killing two people! That's life in prison! Jesus!"

Emily listened, terrified but alert. The man who had shot her parents sounded bright, an articulate murderer. She would remember his voice for the rest of her life.

"Where's the daughter?" said the second man. "They have a kid, you said. Where's the kid?"

"What difference does it make?" said the shooter. "Just grab what you can and get the hell out."

"I'm not grabbing anything," said the third man. "This is not cool, Frank, not cool at all. I'm outa here."

So off the third man ran, down the stairs and out the back door. Emily committed the killer's name to memory: Frank. Well-spoken, brutal, murderous Frank. Unconcerned with her whereabouts, for even if they found her, he would simply kill her as well.

"You running scared, too?" the man named Frank said to the second burglar. Getting no response, he said, "Just go through this room with me. There's jewels, I'm sure of it, money. Check the wall pictures, there might be a safe in back."

The two men began rummaging through her parents' room, opening drawers. There was a large jewelry box inside her mother's armoire, and she could hear him throwing it open, grabbing the jewelry inside. There was also a watch box where her father kept one of his prize possessions, an antique Waltham pocket watch his great-grandfather had owned. His great-grandfather had been a train conductor, and the watch had a steam engine engraved on it. He'd never had it appraised and considered its value to be sentimental, but the watch was authentic and, had he researched it, would have fetched several hundred dollars at the time. Frank had no idea of the watch's worth, but there was something about it that caught his eye, something that made him want to keep it, which is what he ultimately did and why he ultimately died.

Justice took its time, she thought, remembering the watch. Justice delayed was not justice denied, as the famous quote had it. Not at all.

Justice delayed was justice perfected, savored like the taste of something one would only taste once.

The men might have found little Emily in the closet had a distant siren not spooked them. People intruding into other people's homes tend to be on edge, and when they heard the siren they glanced at each other, a wordless communication Emily did not see. They grabbed what few things they'd taken and fled down the stairs and out the door. She waited for what seemed hours, although it was only about fifteen minutes, then she crept out of the closet, walked to the phone on the nightstand and, standing numbly over her father's dead body, dialed 911.

Emily went to live with her mother's sister and her husband in Santa Barbara after "the tragedy", as everyone called it. She did not get along with her Aunt Susan, and was frightened by her Uncle Joseph, a man who was even more stern with his adopted daughter than he was with his own two. Emily always had the feeling living with them that she'd been thrust into their midst, taken in because, well, somebody had to, and that she was damaged goods. What they never knew – what no one else ever knew – was that she'd been in the closet and seen the cold-blooded murder of her parents. She believed the reason she has not told the police was because her life's mission had been set at the instant the first bullet flew; she would spend her life setting the scales back in balance, learning the skills she would need, from replacing her identity to firing a handgun with precision, to bring that circle to its fullness. She did not know when or how, but the time would come; she believed it as surely as religious people believed in God or their reward in an afterlife. Emily would prepare, remain alert, and wait with supreme patience for that fleeting opportunity, that chance of a lifetime, when the great wrong of her life could be righted. For that reason only she had told the police she'd been under her bed, in her own bedroom. For that reason only she had never told anyone about the gun she took from her father's closet when she was allowed back in the house to pack her things. The watch they knew about; its empty case was among the little evidence left behind by the killers. They'd not had enough time to take much more than jewelry and cash from her father's wallet and her mother's purse. And in exchange they had left nothing, no fingerprints, no hastily abandoned burglar's tools. All they'd left behind them was a trail that quickly went cold. But Emily knew: a man named Frank, her father's gun, and the watch no one would really think anything of. A few small things, but truly precious.

After graduating high school, Emily moved to St. Paul to live with her girlfriend at the time. Cassy was from Minneapolis and had met Emily through an ad in a small lesbian magazine. She was also twelve years older than Emily, who, at eighteen, was old enough to make her own decisions but not old enough to make wise ones. Against her aunt and uncle's wishes she packed up her used Mustang and drove to Minnesota, where she enrolled in the University of Minnesota's St. Paul campus and very quickly discovered that sometimes age mattered. Her relationship with Cassy only lasted a year, but Emily liked St. Paul; she enjoyed the distance of the place and the harshness of its winters, and she stayed there.

It was shortly afterward, on her twentieth birthday, she decided to disappear. She had no intention of moving, and it would be easy enough to tell the few friends she had that she was now someone else: changing one's name was not all that uncommon, and she had been telling people various versions of a made-up life since she'd moved to St. Paul. People did not want to hear that her parents had been shot in bed, it was definitely a downer, and the ones who did were beneath her contempt. That was how it came to be that very few people who knew Emily knew her past. She protected it from them, just as she protected her other secrets as she waited patiently to tell them to the only three people who mattered: three men who had intruded into her life and never left. For that, for privacy, for escape, for so many reasons, Emily Lapinksy became Bo Sweetzer. She didn't know where the name came from, only that it was on her lips one early morning as she awoke from a dream in which her father was standing over her and her mother was crying. "Emily," her father kept saying in the dream. He was disappointed in her. She didn't know how she knew that, or why he was disappointed, only that he was. "Emily," he said, shaking his head. She replied, "My name is Bo. My name is Bo." She awoke saying it, and just as surely added, "Bo Sweetzer." She was immediately convinced her father had been disappointed because ten years had passed and no justice had been found. She would bring him peace, she knew then and there. She would be Bo Sweetzer, and she would find a way to end it in the only way it could be ended, even if it took her the rest of her life.

She dropped out of the University and started making jewelry, a pastime she'd had that she connected with the loss in her life. It became a passion, and, to her delight (as much as a lesbian assassin could be delighted), her income. She had never been much for a 9-5 job and within a year she was running a business from a custom catalog. Bo and Behold, jewelry made to order, quickly became a success, but never a huge one. She didn't want the notoriety, nor the pressure of running a business any bigger than could be managed from her apartment. Once the internet came around she launched BoAndBeholdJewelry.com, and would also sell her items on eBay and BidderSweet, online auction websites. It was there, on BidderSweet, one Sunday afternoon as she was looking around, that an alert showed up in her message box. She's had them set up on a dozen sites to let her know when certain items she was interested in became available. It had been a lot of work for nothing, sifting through hundreds of ads for crap, some of them for treasure, but none of them turning up the one thing she wanted. And then, that day, there it was: an antique watch for sale. She looked at the photograph and couldn't believe her eyes. She knew that watch very well, including the dent above the smoke rising from the train's engine. She had caused that dent when her father had let baby Emily hold the watch and she had promptly swung it, slamming it against her crib. He had reminded her of it many times, as a way of saying, "See this? This will always remind me of you as a baby. It's a great dent, I think, one of those dents in life that means something."

She had no idea what he meant at the time, but she understood now: this was indeed a dent in life that meant everything. The seller was an old man in Detroit by the name of Frank. Down on his luck, as she imagined he had probably spent most of his criminal life. But still an intelligent man, a man who knew enough about the value of a watch to keep it. Desperate now, she knew, as he was selling it for a mere $500, a third its current value. He either didn't know, or didn't care, and she had to move quickly. She would not be the only one seeing it, so she immediately emailed him from an anonymous account, one she had set up for exactly this opportunity, explaining she ran a jewelry business and had a client looking for just such a watch. A wealthy client willing to pay $1000, cash. If that was agreeable to Frank from Detroit she would be there the following day. Yes, he wrote back, it was very agreeable, and he took the item down from the auction site. Bo smiled, something she did not do much, and she imagined her father coming to her soon in another dream, telling her she had done well.

She did not like losing herself in reverie. There was danger in the distraction of daydreaming – or in this case, late-night dreaming. She glanced at the clock: eleven forty-five p.m. She hadn't made any judgments yet of this Pride Lodge. She knew what history of the place she had read on its website and was aware the original owners had moved on, one to the hereafter and another to Florida. The only person she'd spoken to since arriving was the desk clerk, Ricki, who told her most people came the next day, Friday. All the better; she wanted to come in under the radar, to get herself into place so she could go unnoticed. She was not a killer, not really, and she had driven all this way (guns did not travel well by airplane) for just one purpose, to put an end to her late-night dreaming and her reveries and let her dead parents know that while little Emily had escaped, the men who did this had not.

She began unpacking the one suitcase she'd brought with her. She lifted out her father's gun, one she had practiced with a thousand times at a Minneapolis firing range and used in real-life, real-time, once in Detroit. It had served her well and she knew it as an extension of her hand. That's exactly how it had felt when she lifted it quickly and smoothly from her purse and aimed it at Frank Grandy. He had been so surprised, so flabbergasted. "You can take the watch. Take my money. I don't have much . . ."

"You don't remember me?" she had said.

He'd looked at her then, clearly not comprehending who she was.

"Oh," she said. "That's right. You never saw me. But I saw you. I was in the closet."

Then he knew. She could see it in his eyes as they widened and he whispered, "The little girl . . ."

"Yes," she said. "The little girl." After some brief negotiation in which he attempted to barter his life for information on his co-criminals, she shot him in the forehead. It hadn't felt good. It hadn't felt anything. She had not smiled. She had simply taken the watch from the case he had it in and left. It was the only thing the police reported stolen, and the very thing Sam Tatum read about that told him they had not escaped the past.

She wasn't sure if she would use the gun again. An ice pick had worked well in Los Angeles, and she may yet find a way to make it look like an accident. There were plenty of stairs here to fall down, a ravine or two to go tumbling into. Ways to die in nature as if nature were the cause. She would have to sleep on it, give herself to that reverie that mostly haunted her, seeking in it a solution. She put away her last pair of slacks, undressed, and slid beneath the covers of her double bed. She reached over and in the last gesture of a long day she turned off the night stand light.

Chapter Four

LONELY BLUE POOL

Kyle always beat the sunrise. He couldn't remember the last time he woke up and saw light outside. He thought it was a form of insomnia; while he had no trouble getting to sleep, his mind sometimes turned on at 3:00 or 4:00 a.m. and would not shut off again. He would try not to disturb Danny as he turned carefully from side to side, doing his best to remain still until the reasonable hour of 5:00, when he would slip out of bed, walk quietly into the kitchen and make his first cup of coffee. He'd used instant for many years but Danny had recently given him a Keurig single-serving machine for his birthday and Kyle had found a new love. So much that they now traveled with the cheapest version of the machines so Kyle could have one of a variety of his favorites wherever they went. He'd never known anyone who traveled with a coffee machine but suspected he wasn't the only one. Hotel coffee was usually weak and half the time the coffee machines didn't work or the maid forgot to leave a fresh packet when she cleaned the room. It was easier to just bring his own.

On this early morning Kyle lay on his back staring up at the ceiling. Their room had a picture window looking out on a hillside, and though it was still dark, Kyle could see the large tree outside Cabin 6 outlined against the slowly lightening sky. He was thinking of their life back in Manhattan and wondering if their cats, Smelly and Leonard, were nestled together in the empty space in bed where Kyle and Danny would normally be. The men slept entwined most nights, Kyle behind Danny, with a cat on each side. Smelly, Kyle's 6-year-old gray tiger, had been named as a kitten when he found her outside his Brooklyn apartment eating from a ripped trash bag. Whatever was in the bag had coated her fur, leaving her with a stench that gave her her name. She was just a tiny, scrawny thing then, a far cry from the 16 pound ball of love she'd become. Danny said she looked like a bowling ball with sticks for legs, and they both worried about her weight. Kyle was determined Smelly would not become diabetic, and after an annual visit to the vet he put her on low-calorie food with a fixed feeding schedule that, after six months, appeared to have failed. She'd lost a quarter pound.

A year after adopting Smelly he met Danny, who had been sharing his life with his three-year-old yellow tabby named Leonard. Leonard was as fit and lithe as a cat who'd spent his life outdoors, even though he had never ventured further out than the hallway. Danny adopted him from Spoiled Brats, a pet store on 49th Street that ran a cat shelter in the back. He had decided that summer he would never meet a man to spend his life with, and a cat was the next best thing. Maybe a better thing. He'd seen Leonard walking around the store trying to decide which of the customers should adopt him, and there Danny was, an obvious and easy mark. Leonard came up to him, just nine months old but already more confident than most humans will ever be, and off he went to live in Gramercy Park. Now they were a family: two men, two cats, and a cursed aquarium where perfectly healthy fish went to die.

Kyle had lived in Brooklyn his thirty years in New York City. He had moved there from Chicago chasing a college sweetheart who had transferred to Columbia from the University of Illinois. David was his name, and he wanted to be a journalist. Columbia J-school, as it's called, was the top destination for anyone wanting to be a serious journalist. Or at least that's what David believed. Kyle had been studying psychology and English literature for no specific reason. He got his B.A., had no interest in either psychology or English literature, and didn't think twice about moving east with the man of his dreams. It was that love, in fact, that had prompted Kyle to come out to his parents. It had filled his heart to bursting and he had the need to declare it to the world, which wasn't something he thought could be done from a closet. His mother wasn't surprised or upset, and while she assured Kyle that his happiness was her only concern, she questioned the wisdom of moving to New York City. She didn't fight it, knowing Kyle would do what Kyle had set his mind to, but neither did she hide the bad feeling she had that youth was more at the bottom of it than love. Kyle's father simply remained as distant as he had always been with his only child. It wasn't so much that he didn't mind, as that he didn't care. For a man who had no other children, Bert Callahan had always been cool to his son. Kyle could never tell if it was because his father sensed something different about him, something he couldn't accept, or if he was simply one of those people who should never have had children. It made telling his father he was moving to New York City to follow a boyfriend a relief to them both.

Kyle soon learned that first loves are called that for a reason: they are not the last. He and David rented an apartment in the Carroll Gardens neighborhood of Brooklyn, and within six months David told him he was too young to give his life to someone; there was too much in the world to see (meaning, Kyle knew, too many men to sleep with) for him to be tied down at twenty-two, it just wouldn't be fair to Kyle. Yes, yes, Kyle said, thank you for thinking of me, I'll be moving out at the end of the month. He kept his promise. He also kept the friendship, and it was to Kyle David turned when his partner was dying from AIDS ten years later, and when David's mother passed away last spring. Their friendship had survived thirty years, and David had already been pegged as Kyle's best man when the time came. It was to Danny's credit that he wasn't jealous, that he understood time was the one thing of true value we can give to one another. He had welcomed David as part of their extended family and had even tried fixing him up a few times with men of their age who dined alone at Margaret's. Nothing had clicked so far, but Kyle and Danny were themselves proof that love did not discriminate by age.

Thirty years, Kyle thought suddenly, swinging his feet out of bed. Time to get a move on before it moves on! He was ready for his coffee.

Danny owned a two-bedroom co-op on the border of Gramercy Park and Murray Hill (also called Curry Hill for all the Indian restaurants on Lexington Avenue). He'd bought it with a loan from his parents twenty-five years ago. No mortgage, low maintenance, a second bedroom he occasionally used as an office, perfect for sharing with Kyle and one of the few pieces of furniture Kyle had kept when he moved in: his father's desk from Highland Park. It was an odd thing to ask for when Bert died and Sally Callahan decided to move to a condo on Chicago's Lake Shore Drive. Why he would want the desk of a man whose death he felt so little about was a mystery, but not one he was interested in exploring with a therapist. He simply asked for the desk and his mother gave it to him. It was pine with knots in the grain, deep sliding drawers and cigarette burns along the right side from when Kyle was a child and his father smoked. It fit perfectly into the spare room that became a shared office, in the apartment he moved into seven months after meeting Danny. His mother had not been surprised about that; Kyle still did what Kyle wanted to do, but Sally Callahan had no trepidation this time. She was as sure of this as Kyle was. Kyle gave up his apartment, gave away all the furniture since there was nowhere to put it in Danny's place, packed up Smelly and told her to get ready to meet her match, a yellow tabby named Leonard she would be sharing her life with, whether she liked it or not.

Kyle could see the sun beginning to rise, spilling early morning light across the landscape. He wanted to go for a walk to the Lodge soon, stopping on the way to see the empty blue pool. It was busy in the summer, a center of activity for Lodge guests, but emptied when the weather turned cold. The empty pool had provided Kyle with one of his best and most-loved photographs, one he called "Lonely Blue Pool." It had been an accident, really, one of those shots he took as he strolled around with a camera slung over his neck, aiming and clicking at anything that might be an interesting shot. It was his method of capturing the surreptitious portrait, the off-guard expressions on people's faces, as well as some striking blurred photographs (he believed in the plasticity of art, the many ways in which it presents and the many ways a single instance of it can be viewed; he liked seeing people cock their heads at a picture trying to figure out not just what the image was, but how he shot it). The day he took the pool photo he'd been walking up the slight hill toward the pool and cabana, when he noticed it was empty and he quickly took several pictures. There were leaves collected at the bottom, gathered by wind and gravity into a brown patch, and there along the deep-end wall was a white ladder that Kyle had used himself to climb from the water last summer. It was happenstance, the luck of the shutter, and the picture had turned out so lovely many people thought it was a painting. But no, it was just Kyle taking one of the thousands of photographs he took. It was one of the first he put on his Tumblr blog, and two years later he'd had two dozen requests for it. He was so flattered by people liking his pictures and calling them his "work" that he didn't charge them – he would simply sign them in the corner and ship them off, asking the recipients to pay postage. But it had been his first inkling that someday, maybe, he could think of taking himself seriously.

Danny wouldn't be awake for another hour. He was an afternoon and evening person, while Kyle had his energy, ideas and focus in the morning. It was their routine that Kyle would get quietly out of bed and have his coffee. At home in their apartment he would leave the bedroom, pulling the door almost closed behind him (but never fully, as the cats did not like closed doors and would either scratch at them or cry all night until someone obeyed them and opened the damn door). He would head to their office room with a second cup of coffee and start in at his computer, either uploading pictures to his blog or sifting another two dozen he'd taken recently, or just reading websites and newspapers. He was also a news junkie, having become more so since he got into the business as Imogene's assistant.

There was no job to get up and go to when they traveled and Kyle had never been someone who could just lie in bed with his mind racing, so he would usually have a primer cup of coffee in the room, then slip out and head to a coffee shop downstairs or across the street from whatever hotel they were in. Here at Pride Lodge he could sit outside in one of the old wooden chairs that lined the walkway in front of the cabins, or he could head up to the Lodge and help himself to one of the newspapers they kept around and a cup of coffee they put out at 6:00 a.m.

This Friday he pulled on his khaki slacks and a sweatshirt, slung his camera around his neck, grabbed his smartphone (he could read his emails before Danny saw him and told him to stop) and headed up the road to the Lodge, by way of the pool.

That was when he saw the commotion: a police cruiser and what looked like an unmarked sedan in the front driveway, an ambulance that had made no noise, which struck Kyle as odd until he learned why, and a small crowd gathered around the deep end of the pool. He hurried up the grass hill to the poolside, having the presence of mind to quickly slip off the lens cap and take several photos as he climbed toward the crowd. Ricki was already there; he may have spent the night at the Lodge, which he did sometimes when they had a busy weekend coming. Sid and Dylan were standing near the edge at the deep end, Dylan with his face buried in Sid's chest, Sid looking down into the pool. They both looked to have just gotten up. Dylan's hair was disheveled and Sid's eyes looked red from sleep. Both men wore jeans, but Sid wore a pajama top under his black leather jacket. Two women Kyle didn't recognize were standing off to the side, one of them texting furiously on her phone. Or maybe she was tweeting whatever it was they'd witnessed. Nothing is private anymore, Kyle thought as he reached the top of the hill and headed toward them.

As the pool came fully into view Kyle looked down into it and stopped, his breath freezing in his chest. There at the bottom of the lonely blue pool, his neck bent so parallel to his shoulders it looked like a stalk that had been broken off, was the body of Teddy Pembroke. He was wearing blue jeans faded nearly white and a blue dress shirt. His tennis shoes were red, his socks black, and his hair had been recently died jet black, no doubt at Happy's suggestion. No 50-year-old man has jet black hair with a bald spot in back and a rapidly receding hairline in front. His horn-rimmed glasses he'd been so fond of now that they'd come back in fashion lay shattered a few inches from his face. His left arm was bent at the elbow, the hand nearly to his lips as if he had suddenly thought of something the instant he died, and there, just a few inches from it, a broken martini glass.

Teddy was the general handyman for Pride Lodge and had held different jobs there over the years. At one point he'd run the Karaoke bar, and he had done a year's stint as the desk manager when Ricki had to go home to Memphis to take care of his ailing mother. For the past two years he had been helping Sid and Dylan upgrade the property, re-carpet the rooms, fix the many little things that had run down over the twenty-five years Pucky and Stu had the place. He had also been Kyle's friend and reached out to him the previous year when he needed to talk to someone about his problems.

"You take a lot of pictures, Kyle," Teddy had said, one afternoon when they were alone in the Lodge's great room.

"I don't know why," Kyle replied. "I think I see the world in images. Even videos, which I don't much care for, are just thousands of single images flashing in front of you."

"Do you ever talk to them?"

"Pardon?"

"The people you take pictures of. I've seen you. Very sly, the way you do that."

Kyle had blushed, having never been caught red handed before – or in this case red faced. He had indeed thought he was sly, clever in a way, getting realistic expressions of the faces of people who had no idea they were being photographed. It was a violation of sorts, he knew, and he was startled that Teddy, of all people, had the goods on him. He had known Teddy as the guy who came into their cabin room if something was broken, the handyman he saw around the property these past five years. But clearly he was an observer, too, and he'd caught Kyle at his own game.

"Well, no," Kyle said, waving Teddy over to the large couch in front of the bay window. Teddy came over and sat down, putting his coffee cup on a coaster on the side stand.

"The point of taking pictures of people when they don't know it, is that they don't know it," Kyle said.

"Yeah, but I bet if you asked them they'd say yes anyway. And then you could talk to them, get to know them a little. The way you do it, you only ever know what you imagine.

Kyle saw Teddy in a different light after that. Not that he had ever assumed Teddy wasn't a man of substance, only that he hadn't considered him the potential friend he became. They were never especially close; that's hard to do when Kyle and Danny lived in Manhattan and Teddy lived at Pride Lodge. They only saw each other three times a year when the couple stayed there, but they emailed and sometimes they spoke on the phone, as they had just two nights before when Teddy told him he would be leaving the Lodge soon but didn't want to discuss it on the phone.

Kyle walked over to the two women who had moved away from the pool's edge. The one busy thumbing the news of a dead body in a pool to her hundreds of Twitter followers didn't look up. She was squat, with a distinctly wide bottom in stone-washed jeans a dark green hoody. Her hair was short, red and curly, and she wore a pair of pink cat-eye glasses, the most striking thing about her. The taller woman had a more evolved sense of style, with navy slacks, a turquoise blouse and a gray p-coat. She stood tall, her posture impeccable, and Kyle pegged her as a professional woman, someone aware of her appearance at all but the least guarded moments. She did not wear glasses, as so many of the Lodge guests did (it went with the demographic), and her hair was just going gray, most of it raven's black and tied loosely back. She nodded at Kyle and extended her hand.

"Eileen," she said, shaking hands. "That's Maggie. Don't mind her, she thinks she's a citizen journalist. Or sixteen, I'm never sure."

Maggie seemed unaware that her companion was talking to anyone, or that Kyle had come into their presence.

"What happened?" Kyle said. "I didn't hear an ambulance."

"There wasn't a life to save, that's my guess," said Eileen. "I mean, he's dead, you can tell that."

Kyle looked down into the pool and just then noticed a woman – a detective, he presumed – kneeling by the body as one paramedic climbed down the pool ladder while a second eased a gurney along from the shallow end.

"It's horrible," Dylan said, coming over to them.

"You saw it?" Kyle asked.

"Nobody saw it! Sid was making his morning rounds and found him. I'm guessing he was drinking and slipped. I kept telling him to stop, you have to stop, Teddy, I just had a feeling it would end badly for him."

"Death by Appletini," said Eileen.

"I like that!" blurted Maggie, momentarily aware of her surroundings, then tweeting what she'd just heard.

Dylan looked at him and discreetly shook his head: this was not something to discuss further in front of Lodge guests. The death alone might mean a change in plans. He had to think, he had to talk to Sid and see what they should do.

Kyle watched as the detective stepped away from the body and allowed the paramedics to set up their gurney and go about removing poor Teddy from the bottom of the lonely blue pool. He realized suddenly that the scene would soon change as the EMT workers removed the body; evidence that was there now might be gone or contaminated simply by being handled. He hurried over to the edge of the pool, aimed his camera down into it with a quick adjustment of the zoom, and took a half dozen photographs in rapid succession, moving very slightly each time to create, once he had the pictures in front of him, a wide, detailed view of the scene in the pool. As he was about to take a shot of Teddy's body being moved to a stretcher, he felt a hand on his shoulder, pulling his arm away from the camera.

"No photographs," said a cop, the one Kyle had not noticed in the turmoil. "You from the news?"

Kyle turned to the officer. He was older and heavy, probably not far from retirement, and Kyle wondered why he would still be a patrol cop. You didn't usually see men of his age out from behind desks. His patrol car identified him as being from the New Hope Police Department. His hair was a gray crew-cut, and his nose was red and pitted as if he'd had a few too many Appletinis himself over the years.

"No," said Kyle. "I'm not in the media. I'm staying here at the Lodge. I just take pictures."

"Well not today, not here," said the cop. And then, to all of them, "Don't go far. Detective Sikorsky is going to want to speak to everyone."

"Is this a murder?" asked Maggie, no doubt hoping for something juicy to share on her social networks.

"It's not for anyone to say," the cop said, "but frankly it looks like too many drinks and a step in the wrong direction."

This, Kyle knew, was not the case. At least, he was as sure of it as he could be, given Teddy's history and the personal things he had shared with Kyle over the last year. Kyle hurried away from the group, back down the hill to Cabin 6 to get Danny out of bed and tell him what was happening. The lonely blue pool wasn't lonely anymore.

Chapter Five

ROOM 202

The woman whose name had once been Emily watched the scene play out poolside from her second-floor window. The sound of the ambulance and police arriving had woken her fully up, even though no sirens had blared. Before then she'd been lying in bed in a half-dream state, remembering the shock on the man's face in Detroit and how sorry he had professed to be, so very sorry for what he believed had been a momentary lapse in judgment. Killing her parents while she cowered in a closet, it seemed, was what he considered a bad split decision. So convinced was he of his own powers of persuasion that he readily gave up the names of the other two men, and while not all three had stayed in contact the connection had never been completely lost. Tracing one to the other would not be difficult and he would in fact be happy to help her, something for which he would need to be alive. She thanked him for the offer and shot him in the head, just like that.

"Oh," she said to his corpse on the couch, his head thrown back with a bullet hole above the left eye, as she slipped her father's watch into her pocket, "I kept the gun, too."

She wished she could say that killing a man was the last thing she could imagine herself doing, but it was the one thing she had imagined every day for thirty years. She had fantasized it, prepared for it, and now, in a shabby apartment in a dilapidated city, she had done it. The only thing that surprised her as she collected her things and wiped down what few finger-prints she may have left, was how plain it felt, how anticlimactic. It was, she realized sadly, as cool and unemotional as it must have been for the man she'd just killed to murder her parents. At least she knew now she could do it, and would do it twice more. She saw that Frank used a laptop and she took that on her way out. She didn't believe there was any way to trace what little correspondence she'd had with this man from an anonymous email account, but she might as well throw his computer in the river for good measure.

She shook off the memories and made a cup of coffee with the machine in her room, then stood by the window and watched the commotion at the pool, standing to the side so no one looking up would see her. She had heard no argument outside the night before or in the pre-dawn, no noise at all, and she wondered how the man managed to die at the bottom of the empty pool without making a sound. She guessed it would be seen as an accident, but she had her doubts about that. It was so clean and neat, with a feeling of deliberateness about it. Could it possibly have something to do with her mission here? Might the hunted be doing some hunting himself? If that was the case, then he knew about his old friends in Detroit and Los Angeles and he was making moves of his own. Good, she thought, blowing on the hot coffee. Let him worry. Worried men make mistakes.

She set her cup on the dresser top and headed to the closet, taking out her clothes for the day, meditating on what an interesting weekend it was going to be.

Chapter Six

CABIN 6

As much as Danny prodded Kyle to leave Imogene and the job behind, he was guilty of always being on duty himself, even if it meant only thinking about the job. He sat at the small round table provided in each room, sipped his own single-serving cup of coffee and reviewed plans for a very special private luncheon at Margaret's Passion the following Wednesday. Margaret was turning 80 and a select who's-who of city politics, entertainment and culture were on the guest list. There would be toasts from Broadway legends as well as the mayor, and the cake was being made by culinary icon Billy Cervette himself, repaying the loyalty he'd had for Margaret since she gave him his start twenty years ago. The list was short – only sixty people – and already there had been rumblings of displeasure from the names left off. Each of them would receive a sincere apology from Margaret, written and sent out by Danny, explaining that it was a space issue, no offense was intended. Margaret's Passion had been famous for years for how difficult it could be to get into, since it only had ten tables of four and ten of two: the math was easy enough, and there was simply no way to accommodate more, as much as she wished there had been since each and every one meant so very much to her. Danny had crafted the apology with exceeding care; it did not do to offend anyone at any point in their career, since a year from now they could be nominated for a Tony or taking an oath of office.

He was drifting off into thoughts of Margaret and how close they'd become since he started working for her. So close he did not mention it to his own mother; while he knew one was his mother and the other his employer, emotions, jealousy among them, were tricky things. Margaret had taken him under her wing, much as she had a young chef named Billy Cervette, but Billy had gone on to international fame while Danny had stayed, spending his work life and a fair amount of his private life one floor down from where Margaret had lived for thirty-five years, fifteen of them as a widow. Why me, Danny wondered, when there must have been others she could have all but adopted. It was the way their personalities clicked. She humored his eccentricities, much the way Kyle did now. She listened patiently to his occasional tirade at something gone wrong in the restaurant, which he would express to her rather than take out on the staff. She had welcomed Kyle into both their lives as if he was the complement to everything Danny was. She understood, too, about the mother issue, and she had always been careful not to give the impression that she misunderstood the boundaries. Danny's aging parents lived in Astoria, and more than once over the last ten years Danny had asked Margaret for advice and she had suggested he speak to his mother. He and Kyle took the N train to Astoria every Sunday for mid-day dinner unless they were travelling. Danny remained sensitive to Eleanor Durban's feelings and left Margaret out of conversation when they were there.

Danny had just finished his coffee when Kyle came into the cabin, his manner flustered and urgent.

"He's dead," Kyle said, taking the camera from around his neck and dropping it onto the bed.

"Who's dead?" asked Danny. "What are you talking about?"

Kyle crossed around the bed and sat on the corner nearest to Danny.

"I should have called him last night. He wasn't right, something was going on, he told me that. Why didn't I just pick up the phone and call?"

"Is this Teddy you're talking about? What do you mean, he's dead?"

Kyle sighed, staring out the window into the woods beyond. He felt as if he were still trying to wake up, that the morning's events had been a dream and if he just closed his eyes tightly enough he would open them to a different reality, one in which he and Danny were having their usual weekend at Pride Lodge and death was no part of it.

"Yes, Teddy," Kyle said. "At the bottom of the pool."

"Drowned?!"

"No! There's no water in it this time of year, they empty it for the winter."

Danny thought about it a moment, imagining poor Teddy falling twelve feet into an empty concrete pool. "That's terrible."

"It wasn't an accident," Kyle declared, standing up suddenly and going to the coffee machine. "That's what they'll say, but I don't believe it."

"You're getting way ahead of things," Danny said. "Why would you think it wasn't an accident?"

"Because of the martini glass," Kyle said. He held his camera out and scanned the photographs he'd just taken at the pool until he found the one that struck him. There at the bottom of the pool, near the drain that had collected leaves, was the broken glass. He hadn't realized what was off about it until he was on his way back to the cabin. "Teddy didn't drink anymore, and he never drank martinis. He was a bourbon man, Danny. If he was going to take a dive off the wagon, he would have done it with something he liked drinking. It just proves that he didn't!"

"Oh," said Danny. He knew about Teddy's struggles with drinking and hated to disillusion Kyle.

"He stopped drinking six months ago," Kyle continued, "precisely because of this sort of thing. He didn't want to die an alcoholic's death. Drunk behind the wheel of a car, killed by someone he picked a fight with in a blackout . . . dead at the bottom of an empty swimming pool. He saw it coming if he didn't stop. Those were his exact words to me. 'I see it coming, Kyle, and it's ugly. I've had enough ugly in my life, I don't want it to end that way.'"

Danny walked over to Kyle and gently put his hand on his shoulder. "I don't want to disappoint you . . ."

Kyle knew what Danny was going to say and stopped him. "He did not relapse, Danny, I know he didn't. He had support, he had his AA meetings, and when he called me the other day about coming here he was sober as a judge, although where anybody got the idea judges were sober . . . I even asked him, Danny. I said, 'You're not going to drink over this, whatever it is, right?' No, no, he was sure of it, he needed his wits about him, he said. I know he didn't drink."

"Can you at least allow for the possibility?" Danny said carefully. "Maybe that was the big news he had and he couldn't bear to tell you on the phone." He saw the hurt in Kyle's expression and wished he didn't have to say this. "I never had anything against Teddy. I didn't know him, and you know I don't make judgments about people I don't know. But his drinking, Kyle . . ."

It was true. Not only did everyone know Teddy from his years at the Lodge, but they all knew Teddy was a drunk. He would get his work done well enough, and the man was universally liked, but there was also an element of pity to how people felt about him. He most often greeted guests with a telltale whiff of bourbon on his breath, and too many times he'd been found passed out on one of the sofas in the Lodge's great room or downstairs in one of the bar's green leather booths. Then, after reaching out to Kyle, who'd done some research and connected Teddy with an AA group in New Hope, he started to get sober. It took time, with a few false starts, but Teddy had been sober for six months when he was found dead that morning. Kyle was convinced of it. Teddy had turned a crucial corner and there was no way in hell he was going to end his life with a broken neck and a shattered martini glass next to him, unless someone else ended it for him.

"I don't really want to go over this again," Kyle said. "I know you didn't like him calling me in the middle of the night –"

"He should have been calling his AA friends at that hour. His sponsor, whatever. You're not part of that circle."

"I was his friend," Kyle said. "That was enough. At least until last night."

"This is not your fault," Danny said. "It was late, too late to return anyone's phone call, they wouldn't expect it."

"No one but Teddy."

"Listen, if you want to beat yourself up over this you can, it's one of your favorite pastimes, but you did not have any part in Teddy's death simply because you didn't call him back last night."

"Fine, fine," Kyle said. "We should get ready and go."

"Where?" asked Danny, thinking for a moment that Kyle wanted to check out and return to Manhattan.

"Up to the Lodge. There's a detective up there. She wants to talk to the guests and staff, anyone who was here when it happened."

"They know when it happened?"

"It happened," Kyle said, taking his coffee cup and heading toward the bathroom, "when Teddy needed someone most and no one was there."

Danny sighed and let it go as Kyle closed the bathroom door behind him. He knew there was no changing Kyle's mind once he had decided to believe something against all evidence – in this case that he could have prevented Teddy's death with a phone call. He knew, too, that Kyle would not stop chewing on this bone until he got to the very marrow of it.

Danny put away the seating chart and menu for Margaret's 80th birthday luncheon and set about preparing for what he suspected was going to be a very long weekend.

Chapter Seven
DETECTIVE SIKORSKY

Detective Linda Sikorsky was the only detective on the New Hope police force. The town's population was a mere 2,525 in the latest census, though it was a well known and popular tourist destination (some who lived there would say trap), and the actual number of bodies in town would increase several fold on warm sunny days. Linda had endured the initial resentment from her colleagues after being promoted into the position two years before, following the retirement of the city's last detective. A few of the others on the force didn't take to the idea of a less senior member of their ranks stepping into a job they thought should go to one of them; add to that some unspoken resentment over the job going to a woman and she had her challenges, to say the least. No one dared say aloud that her gender played a role in any opposition to her, but Linda Sikorsky was no fool. She had a lifetime of experience as a woman in a world that in many ways was still a man's and knew well the subtle discrimination that went on, the doubts and silent skepticism men had about their female colleagues, especially their female superiors.

Some things never change, she thought, finishing notes from her last interview with the desk clerk Ricki . . . what was his last name, she wondered, flipping back through her notepad . . . Hernandez. Ricki

Hernandez. Skittish man, she thought, but not in a guilty way. More hyper than anxious, a subtle but distinct difference. It probably made him good at his various jobs. It must take a tremendous amount of energy, she thought, to be a desk clerk during the day in a busy hotel, or resort, or whatever they called the place, and a restaurant hostess at night. He had explained to her that he was not a drag queen, necessarily, and not transgender or transsexual. He had leaned over and whispered, glancing around to make sure no one could hear him, "I'm a transvestite. I know I'm not supposed to say that, it's very politically incorrect these days, but I like the word. It comes from vestments, clothes, you see. Trans-clothes. It's elegant, really, I don't know why people think it's some kind of bad word." He explained that he liked the particular character he'd made up as the hostess, also conveniently named Ricki. He had invented her, he said, after the woman who used to do the job went ex-gay and just stopped showing up for work. (He knew about the ex-gay part because she had gone on to write a book and cash in as a motivational speaker for self-hating gay people, despite continued sightings of her at Manhattan's Wild Orchid and other well-known lesbian hotspots on the East Coast.) Her name was Leslie and she went by LaLa until she was saved from the homosexual lifestyle and went on a book tour. One afternoon Leslie/LaLa resigned with an angry phone call to Pucky, after not having been to work for a week, and warned him of the danger to his soul. He thanked her and asked Ricki to fill in at the restaurant. Ricki had the idea then and there to do the job as a hostess and had been doing it ever since. He looked wonderful in his gowns and wigs inspired by Ginger from Gilligan's Island and he took a no-camp approach, so successfully that some people new to the Lodge asked who that woman was seating people for dinner, unaware it was the man who had checked them in that afternoon.

Linda Sikorsky was tall, nearly six feet in flat shoes (another reason some of the men at the precinct had been intimidated by her). She was also, as her grandmother would say, a big-boned gal. Someone less kind would say hefty, and she really didn't care what description was used. She thought of herself as ample, plenty, abundant in size, competence and dedication to the job. A formidable foe to any criminal who thought New Hope and its citizens were easy marks. She wore minimal makeup, having always thought it must have been invented by men as a form of torture; her hair was dark blonde and had once been long, but she'd learned to keep it short in police work – one less thing for a bad guy to grab hold of. She wore glasses, but only for reading, and she pushed them up on her nose as Kyle walked over and took the seat across from her.

She'd been interviewing guests and staff at an out of the way table in the restaurant she had chosen strategically for its window view of the pool below. She wanted to gauge the reactions, subtle or obvious, of people who sat across from her and could see where the death had taken place. A lot could be learned from how some averted their gaze, or how hard they tried not to. Normally the restaurant would be serving breakfast, but Dylan had told the twins Austin and Dallas, who had both worked at Pride Lodge since their days of filling in for summer work, to offer people a continental breakfast in the great room. Now in their mid-twenties, their youth was less a novelty than the fact they were identical twins, providing ornamentation as much as table service. They had not been there when the body was found, but did as they were asked and steered the few early morning guests looking for food into the great room.

"Please, have a seat," she said to Kyle, motioning to the chair opposite her at the small table for two. She did not stand or offer her hand. "And you would be?"

"I'm not sure who I would be," Kyle said dryly, "but I am Kyle Callahan."

She smiled so slightly Kyle wasn't sure she had.

"Not the best view," he said, nodding at the window and the pool below. He had brought his camera with him and set it on the table. "It's only been an hour and a half since they took poor Teddy away. Death by shove? Assisted falling?"

"Well, I'm not convinced there's a lot going on here. A man drinks too much near an empty pool . . ."

"It wasn't an accident," he said, and he motioned for Dallas, who had been standing near the entry clearly trying to eavesdrop. "Could I get some coffee?" And to Sikorsky, "Do you mind?"

"Not at all. Then he'll be free to leave the room," she said, tapping her ear to indicate the young man had been listening in.

Dallas scurried away to fetch Kyle's coffee. Kyle wanted to get a good look at this detective, scan her, so to speak, and see what conclusions he might draw, but she wouldn't look down or away. He quickly experienced her unnerving habit of looking directly at him. He assumed she did this with everyone and that it was some kind of interrogation technique meant to unsettle the people she spoke to.

"Mr. Callahan," she said, "why are you so sure this wasn't an accident? Everyone else I've spoken to, including some guests whom you would think didn't know things this personal, has told me he was a drinker. A lush."

"An alcoholic. 'Lush' belongs in the lyrics of a song, not as something to call another person. Teddy was a good man, and he had turned his life around this past year. Well, six months, actually, that's how long he'd been sober. He went in and out of Alcoholics Anonymous for a few months before that."

Linda Sikorsky was not unkind. On the other hand, she was too world-wise and experienced to let emotion and attachment influence her critical thinking. Anyone who watches television will hear that the murderer was "such a nice guy" and "a family man" and that the serial killer finally discovered living two houses down would never, in a thousand years, have been suspected of any such thing by his neighbors.

"People relapse, Mr. Callahan," she said as gently as possible. Clearly this man had been friends with the dead man, and she did consider it an accident at this point, having discovered neither evidence nor motive to think otherwise.

Dallas came gliding up with Kyle's coffee, ending their conversation just long enough for Kyle to nod his thanks and wait for Dallas to head away. When the young man tried to take up his position by the door, Kyle waved at him to keep going, completely out of the restaurant.

"Teddy didn't relapse," he said, leaning in as if Dallas might still be able to hear them. "I know he didn't. We spoke every couple of weeks. He called me just a few days ago very disturbed, saying he was leaving Pride Lodge."

"Maybe he was upset about breaking up with – " and she quickly referenced the notes she'd been taking from interviews – "Happy Corcoran."

Kyle studied her a moment. "I just don't believe Teddy would go over the deep end about Happy. He knew the odds. Teddy was fifty, Happy's just a kid."

"Twenty-five, I believe," she said. "That makes him an adult. What other people think of a twenty-five-year-old being involved with a man twice his age is irrelevant. I was told by more than one person that Happy, whose real name was Happy, by the way, took a liking to Teddy Pembroke not long after he started working here, as a bar back I think."

"Yes, a bar back."

"It sounds more like a kid's summer job to me, but it became a permanent one. Whether their affair was on the rocks or not, I don't know. I do know that Happy has not been seen for three days."

"Surely there's no connection," Kyle said, sounding uncertain.

"We'll have a better idea of that when Happy shows up," said Sikorsky. "Until then I think we're about through here."

"But you haven't asked me anything."

"I don't think you have much to tell me, Mr. Callahan."

"Kyle. And I may not have much to tell you, if you consider a distress message from a dead man last night 'nothing.' He texted me, he was getting frantic. If that's nothing, fine then, but I do have something to *show* you."

Kyle picked up his camera, held it out for the detective to see the photographs he'd taken, and showed her the zoom-in of the martini glass."

"And?" she said, unimpressed with the evidence. "Are you suggesting this was a murder weapon, a martini glass?"

"Yes, and no. It wasn't used to kill him, but it tells me somebody did. You see, Detective, this 'lush' didn't drink martinis. I doubt he'd ever had one in his life. He was a bourbon and whiskey kind of man. Whoever pushed him into the bottom of the pool obviously didn't think anyone would notice."

"I'm trying to be fair here," she said, handing him back the camera. "I've known alcoholics, my uncle among them, who would drink Listerine to get high if nothing else was around. I just can't see this as anything significant. Maybe he had bourbon in a martini glass, maybe that was the only glass on hand when he took it. Did that occur to you?"

It had not occurred to him and Kyle blushed, feeling exposed. He didn't for a moment think Teddy, a creature of habit like just about everyone, would grab a martini glass when he'd been drinking from tumblers for thirty years. She was right, though; all he had were strong suspicions that would not go away as easily as this detective was dismissing them.

"I'm a detective, not a guest here," she said, deliberately softening her tone. "You were friends with Mr. Pembroke, who by all accounts had a serious drinking problem. From the looks of things he fell off the wagon and into an empty swimming pool. I'm sorry your friend is dead, but I've got nothing here to say this was anything but a tragic accident."

"I've told you it wasn't."

"That's not how these things work," she said, closing her notebook and making it clear she was about to finish up and leave. "Aside from his boyfriend taking off, which is likely what happened with this Happy, nothing indicates foul play. It's a terrible, lonely way to die, although I'd guess it was instantaneous."

Kyle had noticed throughout their conversation how nice she seemed, despite keeping a professional distance. He thought, incongruously, that he would like to meet her under different circumstance, to speak to her and photograph her. He caught himself in this flight of fancy and quickly came back to earth.

"That's it?" he said. "You're just going to call it a day, case closed?"

"Yes and no," she said, standing from the table. "I'll be heading out now, but I won't close the case, not yet. The medical examiner needs to determine the cause of death. If it's anything other than from the fall . . . say, drowning in an empty pool . . . that's another story. Even if it is the fall, if some new information comes up, the boyfriend confesses or we find another body, then that's a different ballgame. As mundane as it sounds, an intoxicated fall into a swimming pool may well be the final explanation as well as the simplest one, we'll have to wait and see."

Detective Linda Sikorsky then gathered her notebook and pen, about to leave the resort she had driven past many times but never been to. "By the way," she said, as if a thought had just occurred to her. "How much do you suppose a place like this costs? To buy, I mean."

Kyle thought it was an odd question and wondered if she might be looking for an investment opportunity at a most inappropriate time.

"I've never bought property, I wouldn't have any idea. Dylan and Sid could tell you, they bought it two years ago. Maybe a couple million?"

"Around that," she said, as if she had the figure in mind all along. "Anyway, thank you," and this time she reached out to shake his hand. "Enjoy your stay."

She left him sitting at the table with his coffee and his thoughts. Her parting words, "enjoy your stay," seemed off the mark, given the circumstances, but the situation was awkward all around. Everything about the morning had been either awful, confusing or awkward. What does one say at the end of a police interrogation, though their conversation had been hardly more than a few words, not something anyone would call an interview? And now, the weekend was ahead of them. The ultimate in awkward: a man had died here, in the pool just below the window Kyle was looking out now. Someone known and loved by all (although, if Kyle's instinct was correct, seriously un-loved by someone). What would Sid and Dylan do? Would they send everyone home? Would they cover the front porch in a black mourning sash, or lower the flag to half-mast? What would they tell people? Surely they would tell people, surely they would cancel the Halloween festivities in honor of Teddy? The one thing Kyle knew for certain was that he and Danny would not be leaving for the City. They would stay here as planned, and Kyle would not rest until he could prove to others what he knew for himself: Teddy Pembroke had been murdered.

Chapter Eight

Room 202

Bo Sweetzer had wondered about the detective during their interview. Linda Sikorsky was a looker by anyone's standards, what might have been referred to as Amazonian in less politically self-conscious times. Bo had tried to drop hints, mentioning a local lesbian hangout she'd read about in the New Hope Gay Guide. There had been no reaction from Sikorsky, no tell-tale glance. Maybe people were so much more open now that code between gay people was a lost language. Or, more likely, Sikorsky was straight and didn't know she was being tested. She acknowledged having heard of the bar but never having been there, and she suggested to Bo that an inquiry at the front desk would be more informative. No nonsense, that one, Bo thought, standing at her window and watching the unmarked car drive away.

She had never had a real relationship, including the one that had gotten her from California to Minnesota. That had been puppy love with fangs and had finished the job of hardening her heart. She knew from a few years of therapy in her twenties that her inability to feel was a direct consequence of the trauma she'd experienced watching her parents killed in cold blood. Not the least of it was survivor's guilt: why should she be allowed to go on living when her parents had been brutally murdered? Indeed, she wondered, turning from the window and heading to the clothes closet, exactly who would have allowed it or disallowed it? God? She snorted derisively at the thought. She did not believe in God and had little use for those who did, only insofar as she needed to interact with them for social or business purposes. God had ceased to exist for little Emily the moment that trigger was pulled and she glimpsed her father flying back on the bed. God went silent at the sound of her mother's sudden scream, cut short by a second gunshot. God was for fools and cowards, and she was neither.

She was looking forward to seeing more of this Pride Lodge, of smiling and chatting and blending in as she wove her way into the tapestry of the place. Most of the women here were in pairs, she'd already noticed that. Pairs or groups. It might be the only thing that set her apart: she was a woman alone, a solitary assassin (again she smiled at the word) with only one objective. When she had accomplished that, the mission would be over. There were no other names on her hit list. She had no grudge toward anyone who did not deserve her vengeance, and only three men fit that description. Three men who had broken into her home when she was just ten years old and robbed her of any semblance of a normal life; three men who would pay with their lives. It was that simple, that necessary.

She chose a beige cotton blouse appropriate for the fall weather, and a light gray sweater that would suffice if she decided to walk the property – which she surely would, wanting to refine her plans, to identify places and opportunities. Jeans and black penny loafers finished the outfit, making her look like most of the other women here, and the men, too. Casual wear was like that nowadays, very little gender difference, and that was fine with her. She wanted to be just another flower against the flowered wallpaper.

She laid her clothes on the bed and padded barefoot into the bathroom to get ready for the day. She had completed her interview with the intriguing Detective Sikorsky in the same clothes she'd arrived in the night before; she hadn't expected to be interviewed at all and had not gotten ready before Ricki, the desk clerk, had knocked on her door to tell her the detective wanted to speak to everyone who was at the Lodge that morning.

"Do I have time to shower and change?" she'd asked, not opening the door wide enough for Ricki to enter or even get a good view. She was not hiding anything, but she wasn't comfortable letting anyone closer to her than she wanted them to be.

"I can't say that," he'd said, clearly wanting to move on to the next guest.

Rather than risk losing her turn in line, if there was one, she had simply slipped on her slacks and windbreaker and headed downstairs. It had been a smart move, as she found herself immediately sitting across from Linda Sikorsky, wondering if, had circumstances been completely different from what they were about to become, she might ask the woman out.

The killer and the cop. The thought amused her, even as it reminded her of her essential loneliness. She sighed at life's absurdities, the contrast often found between what was and what one wished could be, and she stepped into the shower.

Chapter Nine

THE SHOW GOES ON

Sid and Dylan both insisted it's what Teddy would want, that canceling the Halloween party and sending the guests home would only make a tragic situation worse.

"We don't even have to tell people," Dylan had said when the two of them were discussing it alone in their suite.

"Excuse me?" Sid had replied, startled at the suggestion they hide Teddy's death. "You honestly think no one who was here this morning is going to talk about it?"

"No, no," said Dylan. "I know they will, they've probably already got it on their Facebook pages. I just mean we don't have to make a signature issue of it. Teddy wouldn't want that any more than he would want us cancelling. It just draws attention to how he died . . . the booze, I mean."

The two Lodge owners then met with the staff mid-morning and everyone agreed the show would go on. They would not refuse to discuss Teddy's death, and they certainly wouldn't pretend that nothing had happened, but they would leave it to anyone arriving to ask about it or wonder where Teddy was. The guests would make sure they knew anyway. There was nothing they could do to keep them from talking. But they would carry on. This was Teddy's favorite weekend at the Lodge, and to cancel it all, to hang the place in black bunting or some such thing, would only bind the annual weekend to his passing.

"Maybe they're right," Danny said, sipping a hot chocolate as he sat in one of the great room's overstuffed chairs. There were two of them, both a soft, sinking beige, with a matching couch given more color by a large green plaid sham thrown over its back. An empty brown recliner faced the television mounted high in a corner.

Kyle was sitting next to Danny, the chairs angled slightly to face each other, as he watched more guests check in. He had been doing his usual surreptitious picture-taking, the camera at chest angle so no one looking would know he was taking their photograph, the zoom set just right for getting snapshots of incoming guests at the front desk.

"Yes and no," Kyle said, just then clicking the shutter for a shot of two middle-aged men checking in. Kyle didn't know them, but judged from their easy way with each other they were a couple. "I mean, it's kind of unnerving. It's not even noon and everything's back to normal, if you don't count a death, interviews with a homicide detective and a staff meeting to see if they should close the place down."

"Teddy wouldn't want that."

"Does anyone really know what Teddy would want? Maybe it's Sid and Dylan who don't want to lose the money."

"That's cold."

"And having a Halloween party after the death of someone who's worked here for fifteen years isn't?"

"Not the way they see it," Danny said. "Not the way most of the people here are going to see it."

"Right. The show must go on."

"Why are you being like this?" asked Danny. He didn't like it when Kyle was surly, and while the morning's events were more than unsettling, there was nothing anyone could do about it, no way to bring Teddy Pembroke back from the dead.

"I'm being like this because my friend is dead and everyone thinks he took a drunken fall and I don't believe it for an instant."

"Leave that to the police."

"She thinks he fell, too! And if it were true – which it's not – it only makes the whole thing more unseemly! Oh, let's have a party so everyone can get drunk and raise a toast to poor drunken Teddy, poor dead Teddy, the lush at the bottom of the pool."

"We could just leave, you know. We'll check out, tell them it's not for us, and be back to the City by mid-afternoon. Smelly and Leonard would be thrilled. She's gotten too fat, Smelly has, have you noticed?"

"She's always been fat. But fatter, yes, we'll have to watch that. Cats get diabetes just like people. And no, I don't want to check out."

Kyle turned and angled the camera for another quick shot, this one of Diane Haley and her girlfriend, just arrived in an Escalade Kyle had watched them park in the side lot. Diane was in her mid-40s, tall and on the butch side with a platinum crew cut and an impeccable turquoise pantsuit. Over-dressed, but then Diane always was. She owned a very successful hair salon in Princeton called Diane's, of course. You couldn't step through the door for less than $200. She'd been coming to Pride Lodge for years and, Kyle noticed, had managed to stay with the same woman for two of them. Her girlfriend, Cecelia-something, was what used to be termed a lipstick lesbian. Just a few years younger than Diane, she still looked like the high-priced runway model she once was. This was a pair who could not enter a room unnoticed.

"We're staying," said Kyle, clicking the photo and waving as Cecelia instinctively turned toward him at the sound of a camera. "I'll leave when I know the truth."

At that Kyle shifted in his chair and stared wistfully out the window. More people would be coming. Linus Hern, Danny's nemesis in the restaurant business. Linus's favorite person was Linus. He amused himself, entertained himself, engaged himself in intellectual gamesmanship, and thought nothing of saying that Margaret's Passion was on its last table leg, so to speak. Linus had started and sold a string of restaurants, none of them remarkable, all of them profitable enough at sale to leave him floating in cash. He frowned at what he considered boutique establishments like Margaret's, and when it was confirmed he had not been invited to her very high-profile birthday luncheon he'd sniffed, "I didn't know she was still alive." He would be checking in later with a current-issue boy toy and a sycophant or three. The group always booked a cabin, one side for Linus and his "mentee", as he called whatever young man he brought with him, and one side for his yes-men. Fortunately it was the cabin furthest from Kyle and Danny's.

Cowboy Dave, the bartender, would be there by sundown. Marti Martin always came for the big holiday weekends, Fourth of July, Halloween, even Valentine's Day, despite being alone. "What better time to meet a Valentine?" she had said to Kyle last February. He didn't point out to her it hadn't worked yet, but being fond of Marti he hoped to see her checking in one of these times with another woman and a twinkle in her eye.

There would be others, filling up every room the Lodge had to offer. The basement would be turned into one big party space with pumpkins and witches, cobwebs and plastic zombies. Cowboy Dave would serve an endless flow of drinks, assisted by one of the other staff stepping into Happy Corcoran's place; there was always someone available, one of the twins maybe, or Elzbetta when she got off shift waiting tables. Kevin, aka Kevin the Magnificent, karaoke master of ceremonies and tireless self-promoter, would oversee the festivities, and they would all dance the night away.

Kyle sipped his coffee gone cold and watched as Ricki provided just the right amount of professional fawning to guests, smiling and nodding, careful not to be too familiar even if he knew all their secrets. Kyle made a mental note to have a private conversation with Ricki when things slowed down. Ricki may well know something he didn't realize he knew, for unless the killer had already left – and Kyle had reason to believe he had not – he would be there among them this weekend. By the time he and Danny left for New York City, Kyle intended to identify a murderer and gain vindication for his poor dead friend.

Chapter Ten

AN OFFHAND REMARK

It was an offhand remark, the kind no one noticed and that would have been forgotten had it not jarred something in Kyle's memory. He hadn't paid it any mind, either, until he was resting in the cabin and about to read another few pages of a novel based on the fictional exploits of a chamber maid at the court of Mary, Queen of Scots.

Kyle had planned to read and take a nap after lunch. That was his preferred agenda on weekends, holidays and any other day he wasn't working. It had nothing to do with getting older; he had been an avid napper since childhood. First came a good meal, then twenty minutes or so of reading, and finally drifting off to a luxurious sleep. He remembered doing this exact routine at his grandmother's house in Skokie, Illinois. His grandparents had lived there for many years and had raised his father and aunts there. Kyle loved visiting them, his grandmother especially, a plump and spry woman who doted on her grandchildren. His feelings for his grandfather were equally uncomplicated: he didn't much like the man, and he had always assumed there was a connection between the distance he had with his father and the distance he always observed between his father and grandfather. It seemed icy father-son relationships ran in the family. But

Grandma Nonny, she was different. And Kyle had always been her favorite, even if no one said it aloud.

Napping eluded him this Friday afternoon, as did the ability to focus on his book. The anxiety had started that morning with Teddy's death and escalated during lunch, when Kyle and Danny found themselves sitting at a table with the lesbian couple from the pool that morning. There were plenty of other places to sit, no reason whatsoever for the four of them to eat together, but the women walked into the dining room, saw Kyle and Danny looking at their menus, and the tall one, Eileen, said, "Afternoon, gentlemen, Kyle," remembering his name, "mind if we join you?"

Kyle was quickly trying to think of a reason to say no when Danny motioned at one of the two empty chairs at their table and said, but of course, they'd be delighted.

"We don't know them," Kyle whispered.

"That's what makes it interesting," Danny said, just as the women made it to the table.

Typical Danny, Kyle thought. Master schmoozer, glad-hander, always on in social settings. It went with his job and why he was so good at it, but it sometimes led to encounters Kyle would rather not have.

Kyle noticed that the shorter woman, Maggie, wasn't tweeting or texting at the moment, but she kept her right hand poised just above the cell phone hooked on her belt, as if it were a gun holster and she was prepared to draw quickly, firing off messages with the speed of bullets. Both women wore jeans and what looked like plain light blue men's shirts. Kyle noticed Maggie wearing lace-up work boots, better used to walk along metal beams in the sky than hiking hillsides in Pennsylvania. Combined with the pink cat-eye glasses it made for quite a look.

"Where you boys from?" Maggie said, un-holstering her smart phone and setting it on the table as she sat down.

"New York City," Danny said. "How about you?

The women were seated now and Elzbetta, on duty for lunch and dinner, hurried over with two more menus. Elzbetta had the appearance of a young woman who never expected to work where appearances mattered: twenty-eight years old, mid-length yellow hair (for it could not be called blonde) with purple streaks in it, five tiny gold hoops rimming her left ear, a nose stud, and all black clothing: black jeans, black shirt, black shoes.

"I'm Elzbetta," she said to the table, "and I'll be your server today. Probably every day you're here, unless you stay past Sunday. I don't work Monday or Tuesday, in case you were wondering, which I doubt. And no, it's not a nickname for Elizabeth. It'd old-country, Slavic or something. You'd have to ask my mother which old-country, but she's dead and never did tell me. Drinks for anyone? Bar doesn't open 'til two."

The four looked at each other, wondering as much about the overload of information from their waitress as they were about what to order. Kyle thought having alcohol that early in the day was a sign of someone with a problem, which immediately made him think of Teddy.

"Tomato juice please, Elzbetta," answered Eileen, putting just a slight emphasis on the name. "With ice."

Maggie said water was fine, while Kyle and Danny both asked for coffee. Elzbetta turned on her heel and hurried off, writing the drinks down on her order pad.

"Philly," Eileen said, turning to Danny as if there had been no interruption.

"Now we are," Maggie added, sounding none too happy about it.

"Maggie's from a small town in western PA," Eileen explained. "She thinks Philly is the big city. Which it is, but c'mon, New York City? I can't get her to go there with me and we've been together for thirteen years. She's convinced we wouldn't get out alive. And the subways? Like being buried alive, she says, as if she'd know. I miss the Big Apple."

"Does anyone still call it that?" Kyle mused, starting to warm to their company.

"Not for a while, I don't think," Danny said. "It was part of an advertising campaign, like those 'I Love NY' coffee cups with the heart on them. Back in the 70s or 80s when the place was going to hell."

"Well," said Eileen, "Maggie thinks it went to hell and stayed there. I told her it's run by Disney now but she won't believe me."

"What'd you think of that dead guy?" Maggie blurted, abruptly changing the subject. Either she didn't like her phobias being put on display or she had very poor social skills. "There hasn't been anything on the news about it." At that she glanced at her phone, as if news of any importance would set it vibrating.

"Who's going to report it?" asked Eileen. "It was six hours ago."

"To answer your question," Kyle said, "I knew the dead man. He worked here for many years and was a friend of mine, at least the last year or so."

"My mother was an alcoholic," Maggie said. "No good comes of it."

Kyle was wondering what made Maggie think Teddy was an alcoholic and why she would offer up such personal information, when Elzbetta arrived back with their drinks.

The now-foursome placed their lunch orders and continued with their conversation, the rest of it light, about the unseasonably warm weather and the pleasures Philadelphia had to offer, since it was the only place all four of them were familiar with. They watched as the restaurant started filling up with guests from the night before and new arrivals. Much to Danny's displeasure, Linus Hern swept into the room halfway through their meal, deliberately talking loudly so no one would miss his entrance. He had a young man in tow – not the same one he'd come with last year – and only two acolytes this time, fawning over Hern and glancing around to be sure they were looked at.

Linus was an imposing figure even without the ego. He stood six-three and carried himself like a man ten years younger than his sixty-two years. He wore his thinning hair a natural gray and swept back, no doubt the better to expose his face. Danny suspected contacts, since he had never seen Hern with glasses and knew that weakening vision was simply a part of aging. Today Hern was wearing cream cotton pants and a light blue jacket over pink shirt, something that looked more appropriate to spring than fall, but it wouldn't surprise Danny for Linus Hern to expect the seasons to bow to him and not the other way around. The young man gliding close to him was almost an afterthought, but a handsome one. Tanned in October, in tight sky-blue jeans and a Pride Lodge sweatshirt Linus had no doubt bought for him. The party moved en mass to a table well away from them, much to Danny's relief. He knew he would have to encounter Hern face to face at some point this weekend, but the later in their stay the better.

The twins, Austin and Dallas, had changed into their waiter clothes (black pants, white shirt, black vest, a code Elzbetta paid no mind to) and were working the quickly-filling room.

Diane Haley and her beautiful partner took a seat by the window, Diane waving slightly at Kyle. The male couple they'd seen checking in were missing, and there was one woman who had come in and taken a seat by herself. Kyle remembered seeing her pull up in the parking lot last night as he and Danny walked down to the cabin. Something about her struck him: she seemed to be intensely observing everyone and when she saw him looking at her, she looked back, staring, really, until he blushed and looked away.

"We haven't seen you here before," Danny said, continuing the lunch conversation. "Is this your first time?"

"It is indeed," said Eileen. "I knew Dylan back in high school. We were both in the closet, but we knew, ya know? We ended up coming out to each other but no one else, not until our senior year. He took the plunge first, God love him. This was in Philly, he's from there, in case you didn't know."

"I didn't," said Kyle. "I knew he and Sid lived in Long Branch, New Jersey, and they've been together for ten years. They had a big anniversary party last spring. But other than that, no."

"Did pretty damn well for himself," offered Maggie, looking around the room to indicate she meant the Lodge itself.

"I'd say he married well," Eileen said. "Or luckily. Anyway, we lost track for, what, thirty years? And then, Facebook! Just a couple months ago I got a friend request."

"They're not your friends, most of them," said Maggie with slight but noticeable resentment.

"Says the woman who tweets to four hundred followers, perhaps a dozen of whom she actually knows."

"It's a completely different social media."

"Maggie dropped off Facebook," Eileen explained. "A falling out with someone, so she declared it a diabolical corporate plot to get as much information about us as possible and she deleted her account."

"Which is never really deleted," said Maggie. "Nothing's ever truly deleted. It's all data mining."

Eileen rolled her eyes and continued. "Dylan and I have been in touch since then, sometime in the summer. He told me about Pride Lodge, I looked it up and it seemed like a great place to visit."

"And he gets to live here," Maggie said. Then, to Eileen, "You're welcome to buy me a resort."

"As soon as the rich aunt I don't have dies and leaves me a couple million dollars, I'll be happy to."

"Is that what happened?" Danny asked. "Dylan inherited from an aunt?"

"On, no," Eileen said. "Not Dylan. Sid. Bought the place for cash, Dylan said. And just in time! Who knows what a developer would do with this land."

Elzbetta appeared seemingly out of nowhere. "Finished with these?" she said, as she took their empty plates without waiting for an answer.

"I'm still working on mine," Kyle said playfully, his plate empty.

Elzbetta gave him a weary smile and headed off again, her arm piled with dishes.

"Will we see you at the pumpkin carving?" Eileen asked. "I'm told it's the official start of the Halloween fun."

Kyle wondered what fun there could be, considering the day had begun with a man's death. He started to say as much, thought better of it, and just said yes, they would be there that afternoon for the pumpkins, they wouldn't miss it.

You're welcome to buy me a resort. An offhand remark, a few words, information Kyle had not had and would probably never have known without that chance encounter. He gave up any hope of taking a nap and turned to Danny, who'd been reading the current issue of New York magazine in bed next to him.

"It's funny . . . " he said.

"I'm waiting," Danny replied, not taking his eyes off an article on the slate of Oscar hopefuls opening in December.

"The detective asked me an odd question, about how much I thought this place would cost. I didn't give it any thought until lunch, when they said Sid paid cash for it."

"That he inherited from an extremely generous aunt just when Pucky was selling the Lodge. Timing's everything, they say. I imagine Linus Hern would concur. The man has the most uncanny timing – he gets out with the money just in time. Whatever sap he sold the restaurant to goes out of business three months later, and it's nothing to Linus, he's on to the next venture. You'd think investors would have learned by now."

"You're not listening to me," Kyle said. "You're fantasizing a terrible end to a man you shouldn't be wasting your resentment on."

"He's had his eye on Margaret's Passion for some time, you know. He circles, like a vulture."

"What if there was no rich aunt? What if the money came from somewhere else?"

"And Teddy found out and was about to blow the whistle, so they silenced him."

"Yes, exactly!"

"You should take that nap. Your brain's tired. It's got you imagining things."

"Should I call her?"

"Who?"

"Detective Sikorsky."

"I imagine she's pretty good at finding these things out on her own," Danny said. "For that matter, she may already know. After all, she didn't ask how someone could afford to buy Pride Lodge, just how much it might cost."

"Ah, but that's the question, isn't it? How could someone who worked as a bank manager save up a couple million dollars to buy property? And why make up a relative who gave you the money?"

Danny tossed his magazine aside and swung his legs around off the bed. "You could ask them yourself in about twenty minutes. It's almost pumpkin carving time."

Kyle glanced at the dresser clock. Almost two hours had passed since lunch. He would not be taking a nap this afternoon. He sighed and slid off the bed, hoping for answers but still not certain what the questions were.

Chapter Eleven

A TABLE FOR ONE

For a moment she thought the man staring at her knew who she was, then she realized it was impossible. She was a stranger to everyone here, and everyone here a stranger to her. It must be the way she dressed, common enough in a resort filled with gay men and lesbians; or, more likely, she reminded him of someone he knew. That happened a lot. She'd been born with one of those faces that could serve as a template for at least one person in everyone's life. It had happened to her as a girl in Santa Barbara, and again in St. Paul. Anywhere she went, really. Every few months someone would stop her and say, "Don't I know you?" She was the spitting image of their cousin or an old classmate. Once in a great while they actually did know her, and she would lie. "No, sorry, my name's Bo," she would say after they insisted she reminded them of an old acquaintance named Emily. "Bo Sweetzer." She liked the name. Bo. One syllable. Gender-neutral. She knew people assumed it was a nickname, some diminutive of "Barbara" perhaps. It added to the fun.

She glanced at the table for four and saw he had turned his attention back to one of the women. Yes, she assured herself, he could not possibly know anything about her but instead had made the common mistake of appearing to stare when really just lost in thought. Nonetheless, there was something about him, a curiosity she found threatening. She would have to keep an eye on him until she was safely away.

"My name's Austin," the young waiter said, startling her. He'd come up from behind her, but she chastised herself nonetheless for not staying fully aware of her surroundings. Assassins did not make those kinds of mistakes twice. She resolved in the instant to stay vigilant, even as she turned to him and did a double-take.

"I thought your name was Dallas," she said.

"We're twins. But we don't dress alike and he wears his hair shorter. He's also ten pounds heavier than I am, which should be obvious. Are you ready to order?"

"I'll have the usual," Bo said, toying with him.

Austin stared at her, even less amused than he had been, which was not at all. "Maybe my twin brother knows what your usual is, but I'm not him, which I just explained."

"Ah, yes, he's ten pounds heavier. Sorry. Just two eggs over easy, wheat toast, no potatoes. Coffee when you have a chance."

Austin jotted down the order and hurried away, rolling his eyes behind her back: another comic. He knew from working at the Lodge that it takes all kinds.

Pride Lodge, Bo thought. They should have called it Pride Circus. The man Dylan was the ringmaster, she'd seen that already, with the old guy Sid hanging back. Dylan fussed over everything, especially the guests. He told the staff what to do and when, but in a nice way, she'd noticed. Pity.

There was that desk clerk Ricki who looked vaguely familiar from photos she saw on the Lodge corkboard, except in those he was dressed as a woman and holding a restaurant menu. Maybe he, too, had a twin, the place seemed to attract them. She'd met Dallas and Austin and she had watched Elzbetta dashing here and there. Elzbetta had introduced herself briefly when she took Bo to the table, and already Bo was wondering, since it obviously wouldn't work out with the lady cop, if this waitress might be available for a drink. One last for the road, so to speak, when her work here was done. She smiled at the daring of it even as she knew it would likely be an assassin's mistake she could not make even once.

Bo was a lonely woman and knew it. She didn't dwell on it; it was her lot. She had prepared for this mission since she was ten years old and nothing, least of all entanglement with another woman, could interfere. It almost had once, with Cassy and her move to Minnesota that had left her in that cold, bitter landscape, and yet she had stayed. As if fate had intended it all along. She understood cold and bitter. They were what gave her solace through the years as she knew somehow the day would come for action, and it had. She was prepared, and she was remorseless.

She finished her coffee and watched the foursome leave. The man who'd seemed curious about her looked at her again, saw her staring back and quickly looked away. The two men were a couple, that was obvious, as were the women. Pride Lodge, Bo had noticed, attracted a particular clientele: older gay men and lesbians, many of them coupled. She allowed herself just a moment of self-pity, mourning a life she would never know. But it was only a moment's reflection; she did not cry over wistful fantasies, and regret was something she had promised herself never to indulge in.

She thought again of the man who had just left and his unexpected interest in her. Was he a danger in any way? Did he recognize her from somewhere? She doubted both, but would see what she could learn from casual gossip with the desk clerk Ricki. Nervous people eager to chat were always an opportunity. She made a mental note to stop by the desk soon and properly introduce herself, then she left four dollars on the table and headed for her room.

Chapter Twelve

THE MASTER SUITE

Sid Stanhope sat as his desk looking out on the pool below. Some days he felt his age more than others and this was one of them. He would be turning sixty-two next spring, and unlike most people who wondered where the time went, he wondered why it took so long. That can happen to a man on the run, a man with a past who could never be sure it would stay hidden. He thought it had. After the first year, when the three of them hadn't been caught, they all breathed just a little bit easier. Then five years, then ten, until it really did seem that this cold case would stay frozen, buried deep where it would never see the light of day or the warmth of the truth of what they had done. What Frank had done. It was an accident, as much as one could call the killing of two people an accident. The family wasn't supposed to be home. They had stopped their mail delivery, which was how Frank picked the houses to break into. His girlfriend worked at the post office and kept him informed of the families on Los Feliz Boulevard and its surrounding streets. The whole criminal enterprise was only supposed to last a few months, until they had enough between the three of them to move out of law breaking as quickly and quietly as they had moved into it. It was a cash flow problem, nothing more, and no one was supposed to get hurt. The Lapinsky woman had put a hold on the family's mail. She'd been telling everyone they were taking their daughter to London for her tenth birthday, all of them were excited. Then something changed. They were home, in their bedroom. They woke up, and Frank shot them.

Sid found out from the newspaper reports that the daughter had gotten sick. As simple and as dreadful a twist of fate as there could be. She had some kind of bad flu or something and the mother, being a mother, called off the trip. London could wait, she wouldn't drag her poor baby across the Atlantic in a plane, probably making everyone else sick along the way.

The police had already dubbed them "The Los Feliz Gang," even though they didn't know how many men were involved, or if they broke into homes in other neighborhoods. They'd had a successful streak of six houses, with the Lapinsky's being unlucky number seven, and once murder was part of it, everything changed. The burglaries stopped as the three men separated. Frank went East, to Bloomington, Indiana, then moved every few years until he ended up in Detroit. His girlfriend went missing; Frank said she'd gone into hiding, Sid always suspected her bones would never be found. His opinion of Frank had changed from one colored by friendship to one colored by fear. Sam Tatum stuck it out in L.A., keeping his head low and watching over his shoulder a little less every year. And Sid Stanhope went as far east as he could without leaving the continent, first to New York City where he vanished into the seemingly limitless anonymity that great metropolis provided, then, some years later when it felt safe, to New Jersey.

He had been planning on collecting social security next year. The Lodge was bought and paid for, the one truly lucky break of his life. And now all of it was threatened. But by whom? Frank had certainly not robbed and shot himself, and Sam Tatum did not put an ice pick in the back of his own head, much as Sid thought it was about time somebody did, given the seediness of the life Sam had insisted on living. He'd been in a state of rising panic after Sam's death. He needed a plan but had none, with no idea how to protect himself. If he knew who was coming, or even if he could be certain why, he could determine a course of action. But he had no way to be sure if this was connected to the murders in that bedroom thirty years ago. He had searched his memory for any other connection between the three of them, but there wasn't any. And surely no one would be coming after them all these years later for a house they'd simply freed of the few things they could carry and flee? This was revenge, but by whom? And why after all this time?

Sid and Dylan had moved into the set of rooms their predecessors called "The Master Suite" when they relocated to the property shortly after the signing. It wasn't where Sid would have preferred to live: there was something haunted about it, and even after painting and completely redecorating the three joined rooms and installing a new, larger bathroom, he could still feel the presence of Pucky and Stu. Especially Stu. He had concluded the old man's ghost had moved from the steps where they found his body, back into the comfort of the Suite where he had spent so many years puttering and overseeing the business. Sometimes Sid could swear he'd seen Stu standing in the bedroom doorway, but when he blinked the apparition was gone, leaving only a shadow outline that could be explained away as the swaying of an overhead tree limb outside the window or the passing of a cloud.

Whatever the case with Pride Lodge, Sid knew the real haunting was his. He had thought for so long he had escaped his past. There had been no indication for any of them that a case grown so cold had warmed again. No one came around asking questions, no one looked at him too long at the bank or the grocery. The only thing chasing him was his own guilt, and that had dulled over three decades until it was more mild regret, wishing things had not gone wrong that fateful night, but never taking responsibility for those people's deaths. He hadn't brought the gun, hadn't pulled the trigger. He was just a burglar in the wrong house at the wrong time. They had left the girl alive. And the thought literally struck him, like an epiphany or the sudden realization he'd taken a step too many and there was no ground beneath him. He stumbled into it: the girl. But she was ten years old at the time. By now she would be forty, married with a family. Could she have found them? Could she have hired someone to take revenge after all this time? He was trying to get it clear in his mind, trying to envision connections leading from that bedroom thirty years ago to this weekend, when Dylan entered the room.

"Everything's set up," Dylan said, meaning the tables, pumpkins and whatever utensils people would need to carve.

Sid swiveled around in his chair. Sweet Dylan, he thought, watching as the man he called his husband even though they'd not yet married busied himself in the main room. Cheerful Dylan. Accommodating Dylan. Doting, loving, gullible Dylan. Sid felt his usual but brief twinge of guilt thinking of how useful Dylan had been these last ten years. Sid had grown to love Dylan but it had not started out that way. He hadn't wanted to be alone in his old age, and along came Dylan. By that time in his life he was willing to be flexible; that's how he considered it, too, not "settling", but simply being open to whatever shape their relationship took, whatever quirks of Dylan's he would need to adjust to. After ten years he didn't even think about their differences, and it brought him great sadness sitting there to know he might be leaving soon, disappearing once again for a last time.

"Is that what you're wearing?" Dylan asked, nodding at Sid as he got up from the desk.

Sid was in sweat pants and a Pride Lodge t-shirt, both gray and worn. Dylan, meanwhile, was in crisply ironed jeans, black loafers and a green plaid shirt with the cuffs buttoned. Dylan was the more style conscious of the pair and took pains to always look good, however casually he was dressed. At five feet six inches, he was a good two inches shorter than Sid and easily forty pounds lighter. Where everything about Sid was large – his hands, his feet, his head, his shoulders – everything about Dylan was medium-scale. He had taken to dying his hair brown to keep the gray out and he swept it back with gel, giving him an open, inviting face framed with silver half-rimmed glasses. He blinked frequently, the result of a dry eye condition, and it made him seem perpetually curious.

Innocence, thought Sid; that's what I think of when I look at this man. Innocence. He dreaded the thought of breaking Dylan's heart, leaving him alone in rural Pennsylvania, but he was first a survivor and would save himself whatever the cost.

"I don't do pumpkins, you know that," Sid said. "But no, I wouldn't go downstairs dressed like this. Do I ever?"

"I'm just reminding you," said Dylan as he straightened magazines on the coffee table. It was part of a fastidiousness bordering on obsession. He turned to Sid suddenly and asked, "Are we doing the right thing? After Teddy, I mean? Is this all too unseemly?"

Sid went to Dylan and put his large, comforting arms around him. He felt Dylan slump into him, letting his body lean against the older, bigger man.

"Teddy would be completely disappointed if we didn't," Sid said. "And really, do you think he'd want us bringing even more attention to how he died? Some alcoholics just can't make it."

"Most, from what I've read. I just feel so bad for him."

"We all do."

"Oh my God," Dylan said, pulling away. "Who's going to tell Happy? They'd broken up, but still . . ."

"Nobody knows where Happy is," Sid said. "It's not something we can worry about. He'll find out however he finds out. Now let's get ready and go downstairs. I won't carve, but I can watch."

Sid headed for the closet to pick out something appropriate for joining his guests. As he stood flipping through his slacks, he reflected on the timing of it all: Sam's death, someone coming after him, Teddy's drunken fall into the pool. And Happy, of course, but Happy was young and impetuous and had probably just run off for a few days.

Sam's death.

Someone coming after him.

Teddy's drunken fall into the pool.

Sid wondered if there could possibly be a connection, and if anyone else was making it, too. He looked again at Dylan and smiled, even though his heart sank knowing their time together might be cut much shorter than either of them ever imagined.

Chapter Thirteen

ALL THE JACK-O-LANTERNS

There were two main events required for the success of the Halloween weekend at Pride Lodge. One was the costume party on Saturday night, when the lower level karaoke room and the adjacent piano bar were turned into one large dance floor with the busiest bar of the year, and the other was the annual pumpkin carving held in the Lodge's great room. Tables, carvers and pumpkins would spill over onto the porch in good weather or the restaurant if it was raining or just too cold outside. And while some of the guests skipped the pumpkin carving, most showed up and picked out one of several pre-drawn pumpkin designs or, if they were really in the spirit, brought their own pattern.

The pumpkins were lined up on temporary tables set out in a U-shape jutting from the fireplace. There wasn't any fire yet — that would come later in the year — so no one was in danger of running out of the door in flames. Next to each pumpkin was a small serrated metal stickpin used to saw along the lines of the Jack-O-Lantern pattern. There were also several X-Acto knives for the more experienced and determined. Dylan, who oversaw the carving (which was also a contest with first prize being a weekend for two at the Lodge), warned everyone to only use an X-Acto knife if they knew what they were doing and if they were prepared for the loss of blood – the Lodge assumed no liability.

Ricki had displayed the paper patterns along the top of the check-in desk and was offering them up with the occasional suggestion. "That's not you, really, try the witch," or, "This might be a little too complicated for someone of such simple tastes. Here's a cat, it has your name on it." Ricki loved Halloween more than any other time of year at Pride Lodge, so much that he'd temporarily forgotten about poor Teddy and the horrifying events of the morning. He had meant to call that detective and tell her about an argument he'd heard the night before between Sid and Teddy, but it surely meant nothing. Besides, he'd mentioned it to both Kyle and that strange woman, Bo, when each had stopped by the desk after lunch. He had the feeling they were pumping him for information, though he couldn't imagine why, and all he really had to say was that Sid and Teddy had argued. That was nothing new; Sid didn't really like Teddy and only kept him around because of Dylan and the fact Teddy had worked there so long. From things he'd overheard – you can't work the front desk of a place like Pride Lodge and not hear things, that's just the way it was – Sid thought Teddy was a sloppy drunk and Teddy thought Sid was using Dylan, though he couldn't say for what. In the end it was all just scuttlebutt and didn't matter now anyway, in light of the circumstances.

"Linus!" Ricki said, pulling himself back from his thoughts. "How nice to see you!"

It wasn't, really. Nobody who knew Linus Hern was happy to see him, unless they were being paid . . . which, frankly, Ricki was. He proceeded to glance at the pumpkin patterns, deciding which would be the best suggestion for Mr. Hern.

Back in the cabin, Kyle had finally been able to sleep for about twenty minutes before being startled from his nap by a call from Imogene, apologetic to be disturbing him on a vacation but not so bothered as to refrain from it. She swore yet again it was something she would only do in an emergency. Kyle and Danny both knew, however, that the definition of "emergency" when it came to Imogene had a significantly lower thresh-old than it did for most people. It might be anything from misplacing her iPhone to needing a sudden flight to Chicago, which she had long ago shown herself incapable of arranging on her own. This afternoon it was for advice – something she relied heavily on Kyle for and as often as not ignored. She had been approached about a job in Seattle and couldn't decide if she should consider it or dismiss it out of hand.

"You've been with Tokyo Pulse for what, nine months?" he said, wav-ing at Danny to stop rolling his eyes.

"'We,'" she told him. "*We* have been with Tokyo Pulse nine months. You're not thinking of leaving me, are you?"

Her insecurities challenged Kyle more than anything else about her. "Fine, 'we,'" he said. "It's too early to make another move, that's all I meant. And I will be leaving if you move to Seattle. That's not an option for me, not anymore."

"Since I shackled you," Danny said, getting up from the table and head-ing to the bathroom.

"That's my answer then," she said. "No Kyle, no Imogene."

The comment both touched and alarmed Kyle. Imogene had done just fine, in a controlled-chaos sort of way, for years before he came along. The thought of her making decisions based on his ability to stay with her was more responsibility than he wanted.

"Be sure to thank them anyway," he said. "Just to keep that door open, you never know. Forward the email to me so I can add them to your con-tacts, for when you're ready to part ways with me."

He ended the call with her knowing it had been completely unneces-sary, and knowing it was one of the things than endeared her to him. He allowed himself an image of the two of them in twenty years time, Imogene tamed by age but still rebellious, and himself listening to her demands through a hearing aid. He smiled at the thought just as Danny came out of the bathroom completely naked.

"Did the maid forget to leave towels again?" Kyle asked mischievously.

"On my instructions," Danny said, as he walked over to Kyle and stood in front of him.

Kyle began to caress Danny's chest with his fingers, ever so slightly. Danny could be ticklish, and there was a fine line between pleasure and amusement. When things were at their best, there were healthy elements of both. Why, Kyle suddenly wondered, does laughter make sex more fun?

"The tub's full," Danny said, "I think a hot bath on a cold October day is just what the doctor ordered."

Kyle tossed his cell phone aside, hopped off the bed and followed Danny into a cloud of steam.

She wasn't very good in crowds. Even assassins have their weaknesses, she thought, as she fidgeted behind her neck with a small gold crucifix her mother had given her for her sixth birthday. It was among the very few things she had kept throughout her life. She had always believed we leave everything behind anyway for someone else to sort and dispose of; the fewer things we hold onto, the less we'll have to grieve when the time comes. And the time comes for everyone.

After the murders of her parents everything had moved so quickly. Her aunt had come to Los Angeles to identify the bodies, something young Emily thought was ridiculous. Who else would be dead in her parents' bed? Many things were mysterious to her then, including the complete disregard for what a girl of ten may or may not want. She did not want to live with her aunt and the uncle who made her skin crawl. She did not want to be the live-in orphan, which is how she felt and how her new step-sisters treated her. Her mother and aunt had never gotten along, and Emily knew her mother would be upset to know her only child had been shuttled off to Santa Barbara to live with her sister and him. That's how her mother referred to her brother-in-law, simply as "him." Never Joseph, never with anything that could be confused for affection or even respect. Her mother always had suspicions about the man, about how he made his money and his dictatorial way of being a husband and father. Unfortunately, Barbara and Carl Lapinksy thought they had all the time in the world and had neglected to make legal arrangements should something happened to them, which it did. Now they were long gone and one of the few things that remained of their ever having been on the earth was the small gold cross Bo fastened around her neck.

She had been wearing the necklace the night they were killed. Even as a child she only took it off to bathe, and her father jokingly said he was concerned she would become a nun. He mistook her attachment to the crucifix for a devotion to the cross. Emily did not understand the whole Jesus thing and never really even considered the two to be connected, even though she knew many people wore crucifixes as professions of their faith. She had no faith, and she was not a nun. She was a killing machine that had been oiled and ready for three decades. Her surrender to the cross was her surrender to the memory of her parents, in this case her mother, and her complete acceptance of the commitment she had made as she watched the men flee from their home: I will kill you. As odd a thought as that seems for a ten year old cowering in a closet, it was the thought she had and the promise she made. I will kill you. I will find you. I will hunt you down.

Here she was at last, having never known for sure it could come to pass. She had believed it would. She had kept things in place, ready to act. But until she saw the watch for sale she could not have sworn in a court of justice – for that is where she now found herself – that the opportunity would present itself and all her preparation would have been for good. What she was doing was good. What she was doing was right. No innocence would be violated; they had forfeited any claim to innocence when they left two people dead in a bedroom. She had carried out the Court's decree with the men Frank and Sam, and now, once she was finished here, she would return to anonymity. She would replace the smile on her face, so familiar to her friends in St. Paul. She would tell them what a lovely time she'd had in Hawaii, her first trip in years but definitely not her last, so wonderful and relaxing and tropical. And she would close the lid at last – the lid to her past, to her parents' coffins, to the hatred that had fueled her nearly her entire life.

She slipped into her comfortable black loafers, adjusted her expression to be as soft, welcoming and unremarkable as possible, and headed downstairs.

Dylan wasn't able to have a seating arrangement at the tables, that would have been too formal, too deliberate, but he could steer people in the general direction of where he wanted them to be. The real challenge with a group like this was knowing who to keep apart, not who to seat together. Diane Haley, for instance, had been in a Cold War state with Marti Martin for years, ever since Marti stole Diane's girlfriend so long ago neither of them remembered her name. Bad blood tended to stay bad, and no infusion of good will or forced togetherness would change that. The same might be said for Linus and Danny, although Danny wasn't really the grudge holding sort. His dislike for the stuffy restaurateur didn't cross the line into open warfare, but it would still be best not to have them next to each other. Linus enjoyed provocation and could be counted on to throw a flame or two regardless of the best intentions or efforts to ignore him.

As the guests filtered in, Dylan accomplished his manipulation by carrying their Jack-O-Lantern patterns to the tables for them, chatting as he led them to where he thought they should be. He had planned it out ahead of time, knowing, for instance, that Linus would insist on the largest pumpkin in the room while Kyle would want something front-lit for the photographs he was always taking.

Drinks were served to ease the social interaction. Austin, Dallas and Elzbetta saw to that, working on a single pumpkin for the three of them while taking turns filling drink orders. More than one person had said to Dylan that alcohol and knives were probably not a good combination, the meaning of which could be taken in several ways.

By the time Kyle and Danny arrived, Kyle with his ever-present Nikon slung around his neck, everyone was in place and already starting to carve. Diane and Marti were separated by an elderly gentleman from Long Island, a regular customer named Jeremy Johnston who took a bus to the Lodge twice a year for a week's stay. Jeremy was the last person to retire at night, given special privilege to watch the great room's wall-mounted television set well past midnight to accommodate his insomnia. He also had the odd habit of pushing a walker with him everywhere, which would seem natural for a man of 82 if he actually needed it to walk. For Jeremy it was a prop, like a cane might be for a man of an earlier era.

"How you doing, Jerry?" Marti asked when he first approached the table. Marti Martin ran a travel agency that was barely hanging on. Her hair was gray and cropped short, almost military style, and she wore incongruously large, red plastic eyeglasses that made her head look more like a baby's than a grown woman's.

"It's Jeremy," he replied. "You know that, Marti Martin."

"Yes, I do. I'm just checking to make sure you're paying attention."

The old man was indeed paying close attention. That's what he did: he watched everyone. He enjoyed the ruse of the walker. He needed it, to be truthful, since he sometimes lost his balance, but mostly it served as a form of misdirection. People would be paying attention to the walker while he was paying attention to them.

Linus and his man-child were at the end of one table, near the fireplace. Next to them were the two sycophants. Danny recognized one of them and had in fact fired the man from Margaret's Passion just that past June. He had been a new nighttime maitre d', and even though Danny was the day manager, Margaret relied on him for the unpleasant tasks as well as the pleasant ones. The man's name . . . what was it? . . . Fidel? Filio? Filo? . . . Filo had given it his best try but it wasn't good enough. He had been short tempered with some of the diners and had an unwelcome air of superiority the other staff didn't like, even leaving one waitress in tears. He had to go, so off Danny went to the restaurant late one night to tell Filo he wished him well in his future endeavors.

"You remember Phineus!" Linus shouted at Danny as he and Kyle took their seats. "You fired him!"

Phineus was clearly embarrassed and simply smiled in Danny's direction.

Kyle took a few quick photos of the tables with all the guests seated. He saw Maggie and Eileen, the twins, Elzbetta, Ricki at the desk (he never joined in and never explained his reasons), Dylan hurrying around making sure everyone was in place. There were some other guests on the porch, a few Kyle recognized and some he did not. There were also several empty spaces: the pumpkin carving took place on Friday afternoon when people were still arriving. It was a tradition; it had always been on Friday. It also allowed for the judging that night and the Jack-O-Lanterns to be displayed for the rest of the weekend.

Just as Kyle was about to take a picture of the pumpkins on the table in front of them, the woman he'd seen eating alone at lunch took the empty seat to his left. She had short, curly brown hair that reminded him of the late Phoebe Snow. Unlike most of the others at the Lodge she was not wearing blue jeans, instead having on rather elegant black pants, a cream blouse and a gray sweater. He glanced at her and saw she was wearing a crucifix around her neck.

"Hello," she said, seeming to enjoy the sizing up. She extended her hand. "My name's Bo. Bo Sweetzer. You must be Kyle."

He shook her hand and she could tell he was puzzled that she knew his name.

"I asked the desk guy."

"Ricki."

"Yeah, Ricki. I saw you this morning at the pool. My room's above it on the second floor. You're good with a camera."

"Not as good as I'd like to be," Kyle said.

"Yes, he is," Danny interjected. "He's just falsely modest."

"I've never sold anything."

"Because you've never asked to be paid!"

"He's right," Bo said. "You could sell your photographs, absolutely. I've seen your website."

This got his attention. He knew how many people visited his photoblog on any given day; he could track the statistics. It wasn't something he did much, sensing its potential to become an obsession, but every now and then he looked at the numbers. If 500 people looked at AsKyleSeesIt in any 30-day period, he was doing well That this stranger, here for a weekend at Pride Lodge, had not only asked Ricki about him, but taken time to look at his site, was something out of the ordinary. While it was flattering, it was also a little unsettling, as if he'd finally acquired a stalker.

"I used the Lodge's laptop," she said, nodding toward the old battered Dell that was always on a table by the checkerboard. "I'm impressed. Maybe I'll be your first customer."

"First paying customer," Danny said. "He's had quite a few customers." And to Kyle, "You see? It's time to take it —"

"Please don't say it."

"To the next level."

"I hate that phrase. Along with a few others: next level, same page, bandwidth. Do you think we have the bandwidth to carve these pumpkins?"

Elzbetta suddenly appeared between Kyle and Bo. She'd got into costume for the weekend and was dressed this year in a French maid's outfit with an enormous Marie Antoinette wig. The studs were still in her nose and ears and her fingernails were painted black with tiny witches in the middle of each fingernail.

"You did that yourself?" Danny asked, indicating the intricate paintings.

"Kevin," she said, meaning the karaoke host who seemed to have it in an unwritten contract he must be called "the Magnificent," Like Michael Jackson having been called The King of Pop no matter how far down the throne he'd slid. Kevin McGill had been running the evening entertainment at Pride Lodge nearly as long as the Lodge had been in business. He didn't show his face before mid-afternoon, which made Elzbetta's fingernail painting this early in the day something of a rarity.

"He just got in after lunch," Elzbetta said. "He'll be down for dinner. What can I get you to drink?"

"I'll take a martini, vodka, straight up," Danny said.

"There is no such thing as a vodka martini," Elzbetta said. "A true martini is made with gin."

"Then I'll take a fake martini, vodka, straight up. And not the house swill, either."

"I'll have Scotch and water," Kyle said. "Plenty of ice. And whatever Bo's having, our treat."

"Why thank you, that's very nice of you! I'll have club soda, please. Make mine neat."

Elzbetta nodded and hurried off.

Watching her go, Bo said, "Not the costume I'd expect with someone so deliberately rebellious. She seems more the lesbian assassin type to me."

"A lesbian assassin," Jeremy said, having deliberately overheard them. "Sounds like my kinda gal."

Just then Dylan interrupted with several loud hand claps. "Listen up, everybody!," and when a few of the guests kept chatting, "'Everybody' is self-explanatory! It means every single person who can hear me!"

"Does that include Staten Island?" Linus said, to approving laughter from his mini-entourage.

"Each of you has a fresh pumpkin in front of you and the pattern you've chosen or been provided. These pumpkins are sacrificing their lives to provide us with a fabulous weekend, so don't disappoint them! Next to each pumpkin you'll find . . ."

Kyle let Dylan's voice fade into the background, much like the sound of a flight attendant giving survival instructions from the aisle of a crowded plane. He realized he needed before photos of the pumpkins to contrast with the after. He quickly picked up his Nikon from the table and set about taking pictures. He wasn't worried about Dylan calling him out for not paying attention; the man was completely self-absorbed in his own central part of the afternoon's drama. Kyle and Danny would carve one pumpkin together, leaving an extra one. This happened with most of the couples, whether they were involved or just friends. There was something about carving a pumpkin with someone that made it more enjoyable and less tedious; digging out the pattern with what amounted to a flimsy, small saw blade was a lot of work and better divided between two people. He snapped a photo of their pumpkin, then angled his camera for a shot at Bo's. He noticed she had one of the X-act knives resting to the left of her pumpkin.

"I see you're a southpaw," Kyle said to her, commenting on her left-handedness. "And a pro at pumpkin carving! I'd probably cut my finger off using one of those."

"It's for the details," she said, holding up her pattern. It was an intricate sketch of Cinderella's pumpkin carriage being pulled by two horses. Once it was finished and a candle placed inside, the flame would shine through the carriage's windows. "I'm used to detail work. I make jewelry for a living. I also restore old watches."

She reached into her pocket and pulled out her father's pocket watch. Kyle had noticed the gold chain running up out of her pocket to a belt loop.

"This one is very special," she said, showing it to him. "It belonged to my father. I'd have to say it's been my inspiration since I was, oh, ten years old."

Kyle peered at the watch. Even someone not schooled in watches or engraving could see it had been made with care. There was something delicate yet masculine about it, and it made him wonder, as he looked at the fine lines of the train station, how much of the little boy remains in a grown man: trains were something a child played with when he was ten, and built when he was thirty.

"It's lovely," he said. "From what you've said, I take it your father's passed on."

"Oh, yes. He and my mother both. At the same time. A freak accident." She put the watch back in her pocket. "It's not something I talk about. You can see some of my jewelry at my website, if you're interested. BoAndBehold.com. Maybe we could barter, it's the future of commerce, if you listen to twenty-year-olds obsessed with their carbon footprints. Something of mine for a photograph of yours. You could use it to get used to the idea of being paid."

Kyle was beginning to enjoy this woman's company. There was something both inviting and off-putting about her, an unusual combination. He was a people watcher. He had always attributed it to a mix of introversion and curiosity, the essence of a photographer even before he'd ever held a camera. He saw the world, and life, as a series of images, instantaneous and continuous while constantly changing. Almost like one of those small picture books where the image moves as you flip through the pages. Kyle was always watching the image, always observing one moment's connection to the next.

Danny broke his reverie by saying, for the third time, ". . . Earth to Kyle, hello, Kyle?"

Kyle shook off his thoughts and noticed that everyone had started carving, including Bo, who was holding her pattern against her pumpkin and poking pinpricks along the line drawing. Slowly, steadily, one quick saw at a time. Everyone was doing it now.

"You hold the paper, I'll cut," said Danny. "When we get to the witch's broom it's your turn."

A half hour later Danny and Kyle were finished, the table in front of them littered with pumpkin bits. Kyle looked around the room and saw the others either finished or nearing it. Bo had moved on to the X-Acto knife and was painstakingly slicing out the finest details of her carving.

"It all looks amazing!" Dylan said. He was holding a drink by this time, and while he wasn't someone who would indulge too much (bad for his image as well as his business), he wasn't opposed to joining the Lodge's guests in an afternoon cocktail. It was a holiday, after all, or at least as close to an official gay holiday as the year provided.

"Now," Dylan continued. "If I can get everyone to take their pumpkins and line them up around the porch railing – it's wide enough, don't worry – we can get the candles in and as soon as the sun goes down, we'll be a proper haunted house!"

"The ghost of Teddy," Ricki said morosely and not too loudly. Dylan and some of the others clearly heard him. Kyle saw a brief cringe on Dylan's face and was reminded that some people would find it inappropriate they were going on with the weekend at all. But it was Teddy's favorite time at Pride Lodge; there was something to be said for not turning it into a memorial, a weekend period-of-mourning, for someone who would be laughing with the rest of them had his life not ended abruptly.

People started gathering their pumpkins for the short walk outside.

"Let me get some after photos," Kyle said, and he grabbed his camera off the table. He quickly snapped pictures of his and Danny's pumpkin, which, if you tilted your head at a certain angle and closed one eye, looked like a witch on a broom flying across the moon. Then he turned and took a photo of Bo's pumpkin, which reflected her artistic expertise. He knew looking at it that her jewelry would be even more impressive: there was no need to close an eye or cock your head to tell what she had carved. Cinderella herself would ride in this pumpkin! He was about to compliment her when Dylan came quickly up to them, a pumpkin in his arms even though he had not carved one, and said, "Kyle, you've got an eye for these things – come with me and help me arrange all these pumpkins."

Kyle had never been asked to do this before and looked at Danny for his reaction. Danny shrugged and carried their pumpkin himself as the Lodge guests all began to file outside.

The porch was spacious and not closed in. Pucky and Stu, then Dylan and Sid after them, had weighed enclosing it so people could sit out in inclement weather, but having it open to the air and the hill gave it a sense of flowing into the surroundings. There was a porch swing on each end, a bench along the bay window looking into the great room, and two small tables with deck chairs. A waist-high railing encircled it all. People were setting their pumpkins along the railing when Dylan took Kyle by the arm and lead him out into the yard.

"We'll get a better perspective from a distance," he said. "You're a photographer, you know all about perspective."

Kyle followed along as they stepped away from the crowd. It was late afternoon and the sun, while not down, was giving it up for the day. Another hour and they would be lighting the Jack-O'-Lanterns.

Once they were out of earshot of the other guests, Dylan, keeping his eyes on the porch, said to Kyle, "I need to speak to you privately, Kyle. It's about the Lodge. About Sid."

"Why me?" Kyle asked him, uncomfortable with the intimacy. He had known Dylan for the five years he and Danny had been coming here, but they had never been more than cordial.

"Because Teddy trusted you." And then, without looking at Kyle, "I don't believe it was an accident."

"Nor do I, Dylan, but you can't take conjecture to court. If you know anything, you should call the police, speak to that Detective Sikorsky."

"I don't know things for a fact. That's the problem. I only have suspicions at this point, and I wanted to speak to you first. I think I know what Teddy wanted to see you about."

Kyle's head was spinning. He wanted answers as much as anyone, but he'd never thought they might come from Dylan. What benefit could he have in proving a murder on his property? It was the sort of thing that might make people think twice about staying there.

"Come to Clyde's," Dylan said, referring to the downstairs piano bar. "Tonight."

Before Kyle could protest or ask him anything, Dylan headed back toward the porch. "Cinderella in the middle," he said loudly for everyone to hear. "We'll work out to the left and right from there. You're all look-ing amazing! And don't forget to pick your favorite, Ricki has ballots at the front desk!"

Kyle watched him begin to fuss with the pumpkins, as if they had actually just discussed arranging them. He was again struck by the imposi-tion of intimacy, the sharing of a confidence, or at least promising to, that should be shared with the authorities. He decided he would hear Dylan out that night, and depending on what came of it, he would call Detective Sikorsky in the morning. He doubted very much she took weekends off in a homicide case.

Chapter Fourteen

STANLEY AND OLIVER

Kyle was Stanley Laurel, being the taller of the two, and Danny was Oliver Hardy, which he was none too happy about: Hardy was the fat one.

"Just tell yourself he went on Weight Watchers and lost forty pounds," Kyle said, adjusting his bowler hat in the mirror.

"There was no Weight Watchers then," Danny said, applying a moustache while he glanced at a photograph of the old comedy team.

"You're missing the point. There's nothing insulting about going as Oliver Hardy. You're not really him! You're a . . . thinner Oliver Hardy."

"Thanks," Danny said, having caught the hesitation in Kyle's voice. He was a thinner Hardy, for sure, thin enough he had to pad the suit with a pillow tied around his mid-section, but not thin enough to make the costume ridiculous.

About half the guests would dress for dinner, creating a mix in the dining room of people in casual clothes eating their meal with people in Halloween costumes. Some of them were as simple as a magician's cape and wand, while others were elaborate and probably took an hour or two to prepare. The previous year Kyle had come as a scarecrow and Danny as a sultan, complete with a sultan's multi-colored robe and a turban. Kyle had hated his costume and cursed his decision: it was made of straw and burlap, purchased on the internet, and it itched fiercely. He endured it for the weekend but gave it away afterward and vowed never to buy a costume online again. This year they'd spent one Saturday going around to various shops and carefully identifying what they would need to be a convincing Laurel and Hardy. It paid off, if Kyle said so himself, as they looked very much like the people they were impersonating.

"I'm so glad we're not in the City," Danny said. "I'd have been roped into working Margaret's for Halloween crowd control and you'd be dealing with Imogene fretting over every sequin on a fairy costume."

"She's a tube of lipstick this year," Kyle said.

"You know what I mean. If you weren't at her apartment helping her, you'd be on the phone offering reassurance."

The two men were just about ready. Their plans for the night were simply to have dinner, after which Danny would return for some quiet time before bed. He was a people person when he was paid to be, at the restaurant especially, but when they managed to get away by themselves, he preferred to enjoy time reading, or even watching television, anything away from the crowd. Crowds were central to his job and, to some extent, his identity. He needed to keep the boundaries clear, to remind himself that he was not his job. After all, the years were passing ever more quickly and the next thing they knew it would be time for some version of retirement. What then? Would he find himself depressed, sitting in front of a window reliving his life in some kind of internal motion picture show? There was a risk in confusing your work with who you are.

"Danny?" he heard Kyle say, and he realized Kyle had been speaking to him while he sat thinking on the edge of the bed.

"What?"

"What do you suppose he found out, Dylan, and why would he want to talk to me?"

"I'm sorry –"

"I just can't guess what Dylan wants to speak to me about. I told him to call the detective."

"He's probably not sure enough to do that," Danny said. "It's probably still conjecture for him."

"Suspicions."

"Exactly."

"But about what?"

"Well, that's what you're going to find out, Mr. Laurel, when youse 'av yourself a propah convahsation with the man."

Kyle walked over to Danny, leaned down and kissed him. "That's the spirit."

"I hate Halloween."

"You don't hate Halloween, it's your favorite time here, you're just being contrary. Now let's go eat."

Kyle retrieved his camera from the dresser and the two of them headed to the Lodge.

Chapter Fifteen

HAPPINESS IS A WARM GUN

B o sat gently rocking back and forth in the old chair in her room. It wasn't a rocking chair, but she took comfort in the motion. It reminded her of being in her father's lap so many years ago, when he would rock her and tell her stories before putting her to bed. Now, over thirty years later, it was his gun she took comfort in, caressing it with the fingers of her left hand. Her shooting hand.

It's funny, the things we forget in a moment of crisis and chaos. Her father had kept the gun in a case in the closet, yet when he needed it he neglected it, choosing instead to hurry his daughter into hiding, to protect her and take his chances hand-to-hand. She supposed he had never expected to have to aim a gun at anyone, let alone pull the trigger. He wasn't a gun man; her parents weren't gun people. He'd simply had it as a precaution, like a life preserver that gathered dust inside a boat and was never worn. She had no idea what had gone through his mind in those seconds, if he had suddenly remembered the gun was in the closet with his ten year old child and it was too late; he would not risk exposing her to get the one thing that could have saved them. And the timing, too, all of it happening so fast.

Bo watched in horror as the man stepped into the bedroom and promptly shot her father, then her mother. Bang, bang, just like that. She didn't know why she hadn't screamed, or at least sucked her breath in so loudly it would give her away. But she hadn't. She had stayed fixated on the horror. And then, when she was gathering her things to move to Santa Barbara and be raised by strangers called a family, she had taken the gun. The police hadn't found it; they hadn't been looking for any such thing. This was a burglary gone wrong; what you saw was what you got. So the gun had still been in the closet when she came to pack, and she had kept it with her all these years. Not only kept it with her, but learned to shoot it, and shoot it well. Which made it that much sadder knowing she would have to discard it, leave it rusting at the bottom of the Delaware River when she left this place, having put it to its only good use.

Bo believed in coincidence. She had no patience for people who said there was no such thing. She simply considered it the universe putting what otherwise seemed random into some kind of order. Thus, had she not been paying attention that day, she would not have seen the watch for sale on BidderSweet. Had she not seen the watch, she would not have made her way to Detroit and used the very same gun she now felt pressing lightly on her lap to lower the volume of the voices that had been crying for justice in her head all those years. For that matter, had she not gotten sick, she and her parents would have been on a flight to London and everything about her life, absolutely everything, would be different. Surely this is the very definition of coincidence, with all its good fortune and its tragedy.

She stopped rocking. She got up and carefully slipped the gun in a dresser drawer, beneath her sweater and jeans. She would head downstairs for dinner soon. She didn't want to go and would prefer to focus on her objective, plus her appetite had vanished as her anxiety slowly increased, but she knew appearance was reality. She had another day and night to go before slipping away; not showing up was the very way to draw attention to herself. She didn't know if the custom here was to wear costumes for dinner and she didn't want to do that anyway, so she would join the other Lodge guests as herself, the best costume of all.

For Saturday night's main event she had brought a cat costume that she purchased for $40 at a store along the way from Minnesota. It came in a box, that's how cheap it was and how easily thrown away when this was over. Cats were patient, cats were predators, and as silly as it seemed, she took some pleasure in being a cat that had come to claim the canary. The old man, the one named Sid.

Well, Sid, she thought, glancing out the window at the night sky, I'm here, and the cage you've been hiding in won't save you.

Chapter Sixteen

THE MASTER SUITE

S id was disappointed with himself; he was not a man to panic, never had been. Even when the heat had been greatest, just after the murders, he'd been the one to remain calm. The fool Frank had shot that couple and the next day it was all over the news. Monsters kill parents, leave little girl alive. They shouldn't have killed anyone, but if that was the way it played out they should not have left a witness. Not that she'd done the cops any good. All they had were three anonymous men and a dead couple. They'd been very careful up until then, no fingerprints, nothing to trace. The mail connection, sure, but by the time the police put that together in some little "ah-ha" moment, the three of them would be long gone and Frank's girlfriend from the post office would be as well. Sid felt bad for her, even though there'd never been any proof Frank got rid of her, but if you play with fire you will surely be burnt. She had cast her lot with a sociopath, they all had, and look what it had cost them. Leaving his life a second time, vanishing again, would be emotionally difficult but not impossible. He didn't have that many years left and he was not about to spend them behind bars or, worse, in an early grave.

He had no idea who was after him but he knew it was connected to the girl. She was behind this. She must have hired someone to hunt them down. An expensive proposition, given the amount of money someone this professional would charge. Two murders with a third on the way? Could it be? Might the little girl they'd missed while she cowered in her parents' closet have found them thirty years later and still hated them enough to send a killer after them? Or had she simply never stopped hating them and bided her time until an opportunity came, the recognition of a face in a crowd . . . or a watch.

He was sitting at his desk as the sun slowly set to the west. It was that time of day, the gloaming some called it, when the landscape fell to the slowly lengthening cape of night. His knees were bothering him, especially the left one. He wanted to beg off dinner but knew Dylan would be disappointed. Appearances, Sid, appearances. They all come here, they pay good money, we want them back. Passing on the pumpkin carving was okay, but joining for dinner was a must. In a few minutes he would change into his nice slacks and a cardigan, slide his feet into his tan penny loafers, the ones with dimes in them, and make his way downstairs. But first he wanted to see something.

He went online and typed in the dead couple's name. "Lapinksy murder Los Feliz 1981." News that old might well not be online, but a dogged reporter – for she must have been dogged to chase this old hound down – had done a "where are they now" piece for the Los Angeles Times over a decade ago: where was the little girl now, on the twentieth anniversary of the unsolved murders that had rocked the tony neighborhood of Los Feliz. He began to read the article, only available because it had been referenced from another website, and saw that the reporter had been stymied as well. Emily Lapinsky had ceased to exist. She'd left Santa Barbara for Minnesota and vanished.

Minnesota . . . Minnesota . . . didn't he hear Ricki talking to one of the guests who said she was from Minnesota?

He read on and was thankful the reporter was as determined as she was. She found Emily living in St. Paul, designing jewelry she sold on the internet. Her name was now Bo, Bo Sweetzer. Bo did not give interviews, the reporter discovered. Bo denied being or knowing anyone named Emily Lapinsky.

Interesting, Sid thought, as he scanned the now-forty-year-old woman's website, BoAndBeholdJewerly.com. Very good at what she did. The pieces on display were stunning and clearly custom made, as well as very expensive. Also of considerable interest, she was good at not having photos of herself, anywhere. There were none on the website, and it was only by spending ten minutes jumping from one hyperlink to another that Sid finally found a picture of young Emily, now all grown up Bo. She was at an art gallery opening, part of the background, but she'd been identified in the text and that is what snared her. It wasn't a great photograph, but it was good enough for Sid to recognize her as the woman in Room 202.

So she hadn't hired anyone, he thought, feeling a newfound respect for this woman as well as a growing apprehension. And while it was only conjecture at this point, he pondered how much determination it must have taken to vanish, to become not only another person, but a person on a mission, to wait and plan and when the chance came, to strike.

He erased his search history, something he'd been doing since that snoop Teddy started looking into things that were none of his business, and turned off his computer. It was time for dinner, time to greet the guests with a particular one in mind.

Chapter Seventeen

AN INTIMATE ENCOUNTER

O ne of Dylan's greatest strengths at running the Lodge, a strength he would otherwise never have known he had, was his insistence on treating the guests as if they were visitors to his own home, which they were. This was just a very large house and the visitors numbered in the dozens. Fifty-six to be exact, not counting the staff and the locals who came for dinner and the downstairs bars, swelling the annual Halloween party to well over a hundred. Dylan would accommodate anyone who wanted to dine with just a special someone, or friends who'd come together, seating them at a table for four, but he also enjoyed setting up tables for six or eight and mixing it up. He got the idea from a cruise he'd taken with Sid some years before, where passengers sit with people they'd just met at the dining table their first night and get to know one another over the course of the cruise. Granted, it didn't always work out perfectly, and occasionally table mates didn't like each other, or they would stop coming to the main seating and eat elsewhere on the ship, but for the most part it was an effective social mixer, and that's what Dylan was all about. Mixing it up, keeping it interesting for the guests, doing everything he could to make sure they'd be back.

Friday night in the dining room was always busy, and on a special weekend it could become chaotic, at least for the wait staff, cooks and extra help that had to be brought in. Ricki had transformed himself into a hostess in a shimmering red sheath dress and red hair bigger and wider than his shoulders. When Kyle and Danny made their first visit to Pride Lodge, neither one of them had realized that Ricki who had checked them was the same Ricki who seated them for dinner. He wouldn't stay that way all night, changing back to jeans and a sweatshirt before heading downstairs for a night cap and a song at Clyde's piano. The music was provided by one of two or three local musicians who took turns headlining. Legend had it the bar was named after the first piano player in the joint, an old woman who called herself Clyde and who died at the piano one Saturday night from an aneurism.

Also in attendance tonight was Kevin the Magnificent, rested from an afternoon nap. He lived in Stockton with his mother in a house along the Delaware River she'd owned with her late husband since the 1950s. It wasn't grand, but its view of the river was spectacular, and, since Kevin was the only child, he saw no reason to move away. Mom was close to 90 and Kevin expected to soon be living alone. So there he stayed, and every weekend he would check into the Lodge, same room that he sometimes shared with one or two of the staff if things went on too long or they drank too much to drive home. Most recently his roommate had been Happy, and Kevin, though he'd not said anything, suspected something ugly had happened to him. Happy was a good kid, with the emphasis on 'kid.' He was legally an adult, but most people were still wet behind the ears at that age, still inexperienced in the survival techniques that saw one into one's 50s and beyond.

Kevin was filling in at the main desk while Ricki seated people. It wasn't his job, nor had he been asked to help out, but he was in a good mood and this was the busiest weekend of the year. He was wearing a sheep costume with a Bo-Peep doll under his arm. Kyle waved as he and Danny came into the Lodge. The temperature had dropped considerably from the night before, and it had made Kyle think of something that had slipped all their minds that morning: Teddy hadn't been dressed for a chilly October

night. Even someone who was drunk — if that had been the case — had the
sense to put on a sweater or a jacket in late October. But there they'd found
him at the bottom of the pool, in loafers without socks and a button-down
blue striped shirt, with a shattered martini glass by his hand. It made no
sense, none of it did, and he hoped his meeting with Dylan later that night
would clear some things up, or give him enough reason to call the detective. Forty-eight hours, wasn't that what they said on all those cop shows?
Forty-eight hours and the case begins to go cold. He wouldn't even be here
forty-eight hours from now; things had to move quickly if they were going
to move at all.

Danny knew Dylan's modus operandi by now and when Dylan glided
over to seat them Danny deliberately waved at Eileen, who was sitting by
herself at a large table near a window. Ricki had his hands full with a group
of women who'd already started drinking at the tiny restaurant bar and
kept wanting to change tables, very loudly.

"Eileen!" Danny called out, "How about some company?"

Dylan frowned. He had wanted to seat them with some newcomers,
determined to replicate his cruise experience regardless of its effectiveness
on dry land.

"Please," Dylan said to them, declining to walk them over. "Enjoy."

Kyle and Danny made their way over to the table for six where Eileen
was halfway through a glass of white wine. She was dressed as a scarecrow,
and it looked like the exact costume, burlap and all, that Kyle had worn
the year before.

"Ouch," Kyle said, taking a seat to Eileen's right, with Danny between
them.

She knew he was talking about her costume, and said, "Never again.
The scarecrow was the one without a brain, right? He'd have to be brain-
less to wear this damn thing."

"But it was cheap," they both said, and laughed.

"You get what you pay for," Kyle said. "Where's Maggie?"

"I think her battery went dead. You spend that much time on a
smart phone or iThing or whatever and you don't last long, constantly
with the re-charging. So that's what she's doing, watching CSI or NCIS or

XYZ-something reruns on television. Which one of you is Laurel, by the way? I never could keep them straight."

"Oliver Hardy was the short, fat one," Danny said, "Does that help?"

"Hardy was taller, actually," Kyle said, "and you're not fat. There's a pillow in there, remember."

Dallas – or was it Austin? – suddenly appeared across from them with a pen and order pad in hand to take their drink orders. He was dressed, Kyle guessed, as a Chimney sweep, with black high-water jeans and a t-shirt streaked with charcoal, as was his face. He had on red suspenders, which Kyle didn't think were part of the chimney sweep look, but it didn't matter. He looked at the waiter a moment too long.

"Austin," the young waiter said, knowing Kyle was trying to decide which of the twins he was. "You'll have an easy time of it tonight. Dallas is David Bowie with the lightning bolt on his face. I think it's so forty years ago, but whatever."

"Sure," Eileen said. "Chimney sweeps are so . . . a day ago."

"Timeless is the word. What can I get you to drink?"

Kyle ordered a Bloody Mary and Danny a vodka martini, dirty with olives. Austin hurried off as quickly and quietly as he'd arrived and the three of them got back to their conversation.

Just then Linus Hern showed up, and, like Kyle and Danny, he ignored Dylan's attempt to seat him, his boyfriend and his two hangers-on at the large table for eight. Danny thought it was odd, since the biggest table in the room had the appearance of being where the captain ate – whoever that captain was and whatever ship he was sailing. For Linus to turn down a place at the center of attention seemed unlike him, until Danny remembered that Linus was always the center of attention, it mattered not where he sat.

The group's trajectory brought them past Kyle and Danny's table. Linus was dressed as someone out of the Matrix movies, complete with sweeping black coat that ran from his buttoned collar down to his black boots. His boyfriend was wearing a collar as well, but studded, and Danny took it as an indication of what the pair did behind closed doors. Aside from the collar, the handsome youth was wearing a suit, as one might to a fine restaurant. The two sycophants appeared to be Munchkins representing a Lollipop Guild from Hell.

As they floated by the table Linus stopped in front of Danny. Danny eyed him quickly and said, "No costume this year?"

Linus chuckled. "You're very amusing, Mr. Durban. This," he said, indicating his companion in the studded collar, "is Carlos, remember the name. Phineus you've met."

"I fired him, as you told the room earlier."

"Yes, you fired him. And this is Henry. Not nearly as distinct a name as Phineus, but with its own rich history. Now if you'll excuse us, Carlos is a feng shui expert and said this table's toxic."

"It's nice to meet you all," Kyle said. He secretly enjoyed encounters between Linus and Danny.

"The pleasure's all yours," Linus said dryly. Then he leaned down just a bit and said to Danny, "Tell Margaret happy birthday for me. Eighty is quite an accomplishment. She can't have many left."

"I'll give her your regards," Danny said. "I know how much you mean to her."

"So much I wasn't invited."

"It's a small venue, nothing personal."

"Not at all," Linus said. "Not at all. I'm sure she'll remember me for her ninetieth. Or maybe not."

The Munchkins chuckled slightly. Carlos the collar boy didn't seem to get it and just looked bored.

"We'll see you later at the bar?" Linus said.

"He'll be asleep," Kyle interjected. "Beauty rest, Linus, something you could use more of."

"Oh I did forget you're just about as entertaining as your husband. You are married, aren't you? New York permits it now."

"It's in the planning," Danny said. "Don't worry, you'll be the last to know."

The sparring had run its course, the verbal fencing having left a prick or two but drawn no blood. It was time to get on with the evening, something they all realized and silently agreed on as Linus nodded goodbye and took his troupe to a table in the corner.

"Who was that?" Eileen asked, having stayed quiet through the exchange.

"The Creature from the Chelsea Lagoon," Danny replied. "No one to be concerned with."

The restaurant was filling up by then and Kyle was wondering if they might be joined by some strangers when Bo walked into the restaurant, spotted them and came over. "May I?" she asked.

They all nodded. Kyle knew people often formed clusters at extended gatherings. It seemed natural to gravitate toward a few other guests as a way of increasing the comfort level and having reliable conversation partners when they all knew they would be there for a weekend.

"To costume or not to costume," Bo said as she took one of the two remaining seats. "I decided not to. I'd rather surprise everyone tomorrow night and walk away with the prize."

"There's a prize?" Eileen asked, waving across the room at Austin to let him know they had another person at the table.

"The prize is for the pumpkin," Danny said. "I don't think they give another one for costume, do they?"

"We haven't stayed that late to find out," Kyle said.

"We should this year."

"Fine. You'll be sleeping in a booth by then but we can set our sights high.

Bo picked up one of the menus and glanced at it. It hadn't changed since Kyle and Danny had been there in the spring, or, for that matter, since Pucky had sold the place to Sid and Dylan. They'd hired a new chef and made a few changes, but they had kept the Lodge's long-time success in mind and not fixed what wasn't broken. There were lamb, chicken, fish and vegetarian lasagna dishes as entrees, supplemented with a half dozen choices for sides and appetizers.

"How's the food here?" Bo asked.

"Above average," Danny said.

"He'd know, too," said Kyle. "He manages one of the best restaurants in Manhattan."

"But homey, don't you think?" Danny added. "Margaret's – she's a real person, by the way – it's high-end but not uncomfortably so."

"True, anybody would feel welcome there, providing they can spend a couple hundred dollars for dinner."

"So they come for lunch and only part with half that. It's a bargain."

"You think it's a bargain because we get to eat there for free."

The two women watched, amused, as Kyle and Danny mildly bickered over Margaret's Passion.

Eileen suddenly jumped at a hand on her shoulder. Sid had come up to the table unseen and unheard. He was wearing gray trousers and a navy jacket over his sweater, looking unusually dapper, like the proprietor of a guest lodge he was.

"Kyle," he said, his voice low and full. It had a soothing depth to it, and Kyle sensed that Sid had deliberately adjusted his voice.

"Sid," Danny answered, "It's going great, you look full."

"Me or the Lodge?" Sid said, following it with an affected laugh. "Halloween is the big event here every year, you know that. It was falling off some in Pucky's last year, he just wasn't up to it and it made people . . . sad, I suppose. Quite a few stayed away last year, but it was so good you and Kyle came. I know it meant a lot to Pucky. I heard he might be coming."

"Really?" Kyle said, pleasantly surprised.

"Yes, but not staying here. We'd know, of course. Too painful for him I'd guess."

"Who's Pucky?" asked Bo. She was smiling, but it was as artificial as Sid's voice. She was staring at him and something told her he hadn't come to their table by chance.

"May I?" Sid said, nodding at the last available seat. No one objected, and in a moment Sid was sitting with them, next to the woman who had come here to kill him. "Pucky Green was the owner of Pride Lodge, along with his partner Stu Patterson, for twenty-three years? Twenty-five? They built it up from an old Inn that was about to be torn down. Then two years ago poor Stu died from a heart attack on the steps to the pool."

"That's a very unlucky pool," Bo said. "Maybe you should fill it in."

Kyle noticed a tension between the Lodge owner and the jewelry maker. There wasn't any reason for it he knew of, and he wondered, watching and listening to them, if Bo was someone who simply didn't care for men. But that didn't jibe, since she'd been very friendly with him. And then he thought it might simply be a case of clashing personas; if there was love at first sight, there was certainly dislike at first sight.

"Do you suppose that detective will come back?" Bo asked. "For follow up questions?"

"Why, Bo, it sounds like you're interested in Ms. Sikorsky. Plenty of couples have met here over the years, but I'm not sure she's even family."

Bo blushed, having been seen through so easily, and just as quickly realized he had called her by name. They'd not spoken since she arrived.

"Who mentioned my name to you?"

Sid smiled with all the warmth of a lizard eyeing its meal, and said, "Oh, I make it my business to know all the guests' names. It's the right thing to do." He put his hand out at last, "Sid," he said. "Sid Stanhope, I own Pride Lodge, along with my husband Dylan."

She shook his hand and held it, staring into his eyes. Two could play at the predator game.

"Let's have a table photo," Kyle said. He took the camera from the table and walked around to get a shot of the others.

"But you're not in it!" Eileen protested. "And my hair looks like straw!"

"It is straw," Kyle said. "Besides, I don't take pictures of myself. So everybody just squeeze in a little and smile when I say so."

Sid slid his chair in from one side, Eileen from the other. Bo found herself being pressed against by a man who had been in her house thirty years ago and seen the bodies of her parents, dead in their bed with bullet wounds in their heads. She at once wanted to move away, fearful she would find a knife blade slipped between her ribs, and to move closer, ever closer, to feel his breath on her face as she watched him die.

"Cheese!" Kyle said. They all smiled reflexively and he snapped the picture.

"I should say hello to the others," Sid said, easing back to his place and rising from his chair. "I'm not supposed to play favorites." And then, to Bo, "Not even with someone so charming as yourself. A jewelry maker, no less."

"Yes," she replied, her voice cold. The game was clearly up. "I specialize in pocket watches."

"So I'm told," Sid said. "Well, everyone. I'll head off now and do the meet-n-greet. See you all at the party tomorrow, if not sooner. And don't forget to vote on the pumpkins. There's a high-tech basket with pencils and paper on the front desk. I'm partial to Bo's Cinderella, but I mustn't given anything away, it's not fair."

Sid glanced at her one final time, adjusted his smile, and walked away from the table.

Both Kyle and Danny wanted to say, "What was that?" but neither did. Instead they turned to find Austin back at last with their drinks. Animosity still hung in the air, and Kyle waved it away, telling himself it had just been a strange encounter, nothing more. He put his camera back on the table and sat down.

Chapter Eighteen

A LITTLE NIGHT MUSIC

As Kyle knew he would, Danny declined to go to the bar that night, once they'd settled back into their cabin after dinner. It had long been Danny's habit to retire to their bed shortly after dinner and read books or magazines, all the while with the television on low volume.

This night Danny found a Frasier marathon on the Hallmark Channel. Neither of them were much for situation comedies, but they both appreciated the really well-written ones, and Frasier was in the top tier. Danny had undressed, slipped into the gym shorts he slept in, along with his t-shirt, and nestled under the covers to watch the reruns and eat from a box of chocolates every guest at the Lodge found on their beds when they checked in.

"You're going as Laurel?" Danny said, watching Kyle get ready to head to the piano bar.

"Why not?" Kyle said. "It's more trouble to change clothes. I don't plan on staying long anyway, once I hear what Dylan has to say."

"What do you think's going on? And why get involved? This is something for the police."

Kyle had been lying next to Danny, resting up after dinner, but had got up and started adjusting his clothes in the dresser mirror. "I agree with you, and I have every intention of calling Detective Sikorsky myself if this is more than lurid speculation. He can be lurid, you know. Dylan's got a dramatic streak."

"Death is dramatic."

Kyle glanced at Danny in the mirror.

"There was a death, remember?"

"Of course I remember. And it was a death that might have been prevented if I'd picked up the phone and called Teddy last night."

"Have you thought about that?" Danny asked.

"About what?"

"About what if it was an accident? What if Teddy fell off the wagon and ended up falling in the pool?"

"I don't think that's what happened."

"Because you don't want to think it, Kyle."

"He was sober, I believe that."

"Just don't believe it against the evidence, whatever that turns out to be."

Kyle sighed, knowing Danny was right. He didn't want to believe Teddy had gone over the edge, that he'd thrown away six months of what, Kyle knew, had been hard work and determination to change his life. But it happened, and it happened frequently. Addiction was merciless, and all it took was one sip from a glass or a bottle and someone like Teddy could find himself right back where he started – or even where he ended.

The Lodge was emptying out by the time Kyle got back. He'd lingered in the cabin longer than intended, and when he walked back in he saw the twins and Elzbetta closing up the restaurant. It was after 10:00 pm, and the restaurant had seated its last guest at 9:00. Ricki had changed back into his civilian clothes and was fidgeting behind the check-in desk. Few people would still be arriving at this time of night, but it happened, and the desk was staffed until midnight. Grueling hours, Kyle thought, as he walked into the great room and saw a couple of stragglers playing checkers at a table, and Jeremy Johnson, the ancient sentry, settled in for his night of television watching until well past the witching hour. Jeremy would be the last person standing – or in his case sitting – and was so much of a fixture during his stays that people tended not to notice him; he, however, noticed everything and everyone.

Kyle regretted having kept his Stan Laurel costume on. The suit didn't fit well and the bowler hat was at least a size too small, making it perch on his head rather than fit it.

"What's on tonight, Jeremy?" he said to the old man. Jeremy was wearing pastel striped pajamas, and it was not a costume. This is how he dressed after dinner, for his long stay in the easy chair.

"A couple of Christopher Lee Draculas," Jeremy replied. He had a snifter of brandy sitting on the small stand by his chair. Kyle knew it would be top-of-the line and supplied by Jeremy himself. The old gent may love his visits to Pride Lodge, but there were some things even he was too particular about to leave to his hosts.

"They scared the shit out of me when I was a kid."

"Me, too!" Ricki said from behind the desk. "Maybe I'll join you."

"Off to the bar?" Jeremy asked.

"Normally no, not by myself," Kyle said. "But I thought a nightcap was in order. Danny's asleep right about" – and he looked at his watch – "now."

"Have fun. The kids are a little wild for me, as you know."

By 'kids' Jeremy meant anyone under the age of sixty. Kyle waved to him, noticing the two men playing checkers had never looked up during the exchange, and made his way downstairs.

"Basement" wasn't really a word that described the below-ground level of Pride Lodge. It usually conjured images of house basements with family rooms or exercise setups, washers and dryers and boxes stored away never to be opened. The basement of the Lodge was cavernous, as long and wide as the Lodge itself, and Pucky had had the idea to gut it, renovate it, and launch it as two clubs in one: a piano bar reminiscent of his favorites in New York City, and an adjacent karaoke club.

The following night the clubs would be combined for the annual Halloween blowout, but tonight they still maintained separate identities. He glanced into the karaoke club, christened "Club K" (not, he presumed, a reference to the infamous club drug Ketamine, but to "karaoke"), and saw a dozen people sitting at booths around a central stage area where Kevin was announcing the next singer.

He headed past it down the short hall and was immediately met with the sounds of Pete the Piano Guy playing and singing "Come In From The Rain," the Melissa Manchester, Carole Bayer Sager collaboration that always gave him goose bumps. It was a melancholy song and he knew there wouldn't be too many of those played this weekend.

He entered Clyde's and glanced around. The decor consisted of loveseats, sofas and overstuffed armchairs accompanied by small tables for drinks; a bar area with a dozen stools, and in a corner a baby grand where Pete held court with just his voice, his music sheets, and a giant snifter as a tip jar. Kyle knew nothing about Pete except that he'd been the main entertainment here since Clyde herself passed on some twenty years ago. He rotated now and then with other local musicians, but Pete was the mainheadliner. The fact that so many of the Lodge's staff and guests had been there for many years made it that much more welcoming. It was, Kyle knew, an old friend to many, and he nodded at Pete when he entered. He noticed Pete had lost weight: the piano player wore a tuxedo, his own gimmick, but Kyle saw it was a much smaller tuxedo than it had been the last time he and Danny were here.

There were probably twenty people in the bar, as Kyle made a quick headcount. Cowboy Dave was bartending, named so for his habit of wearing a cowboy hat even though there was nothing else cowboy about him. He, too, had been a regular presence at Pride Lodge for some years, certainly since before Kyle and Danny had been coming there, and Kyle said hello as he stepped to the bar and ordered a diet cola. He wanted his senses about him tonight and wouldn't allow himself so much as a beer.

"How's it hanging, Kyle?" Dave asked, sliding the soda across to Kyle.

"You'd have to ask Danny that," Kyle said, winking.

"Good to know it still works at our age, ain't it?" Dave said.

Kyle wasn't sure how old Dave was, and he couldn't tell if there was hair under the hat or not; he'd never seen Dave without it. But he looked to be about fifty, and a well-kept fifty at that. The kind of older man who did a hundred sit-ups in the morning while he watched the news.

"Sorry about Happy," Kyle said, sipping his drink.

"Oh, he'll come back," Dave said, and Kyle saw a distress on Dave's face that made him think the older man and the younger one had been more than co-workers. But he knew Happy and Teddy had had something going. In fact, that was what he thought Teddy wanted to talk about and why he was leaving the Lodge. Relationships get very complicated in close quarters.

"I'll have help tomorrow night," Dave said. "Elzbetta for some lesbian vibe, it's always good to have, and the twins. Ricki gets the night to party, it's his turn this year."

Kyle marveled at the planning, execution and sheer work of keeping an operation like the Lodge going. Someone on duty almost twenty-four hours a day. Bartending, the restaurant, it really was quite a daily undertaking.

"I never expected to see her here," Dave said, indicating someone along the wall behind Kyle. "Maybe she's curious. It happens."

Kyle set his drink down, turned around, and was surprised to see Detective Linda Sikorsky sitting alone on a leather loveseat under a low-lit sconce. She saw Kyle looking at her and waved slightly. Kyle took it as an invitation, whether it was or not, and headed over to her.

She looked handsome dressed in civilian clothes. Sky-blue jeans Kyle guessed had been made to look that way with some sort of stone washing; a tan blouse with just a slight frill down the buttons; brown leather loafers. Even in street clothes she projected calm and confidence, and Kyle noticed for the first time her green eyes, made more startling by their obvious intelligence and curiosity. This was a woman who did not miss anything, and he suddenly understood that that's why she was here: the good detective was interested in what she could learn from coming closer to what was very likely the scene of a crime.

"Mr. Callahan," Linda said, patting the cushion next to her. "Have a seat."

Kyle sat down and placed his drink on a side table. "Here for an after dinner drink?" he asked.

"What else would I be here for?"

He saw she was being mischievous.

"I'm not gay, not officially," she said. "But I'm thinking about it. Which is still not why I'm here. I wanted to get a feel for things."

"In a piano bar full of mature patrons."

"At Pride Lodge," she said. "The place has quite a history. I've been reading about it. Did you know it was a farmhouse in the early 1800s?"

"I had no idea."

"Yes, and the man who owned it lost two children and his wife in rapid succession. Influenza. He was heartbroken, left the farm to decay and was never heard from again."

"That explains the whispers of haunting."

She arched an eyebrow and reached for her glass of white wine on a coffee table in front of them.

"Ghosts on the moors, you know."

"More recently," she continued, "what came to be known as 'Pride Lodge' was sold to Sid Stanhope and Dylan Tremblay. Or more accurately sold to one of them with the money to buy it."

"Let me guess," Kyle said. "Sid."

"Yes, Sid," she answered. "Who, most astonishingly, paid cash with the explanation he'd recently inherited it."

"Lucky man, unlucky relative. Nobody wondered about such good fortune?"

"Cash is still king. Questions have a way of never being asked when there's a million dollars on the table. Make that a million-five."

Kyle was as torn as he was intrigued. He considered telling her about Dylan's aside and that he had come here tonight to find out more from the man who, he had just learned, shared his love and life with someone he suspected of criminal activity. But if he told her she would likely get involved, or want to somehow listen in, and he wasn't yet ready to give that up. He also didn't know what it was he'd be giving up: he should wait and hear what Dylan had to tell him, then decide what to do with the information.

"You don't think Teddy fell into the pool by accident, either," he said, feeling a sadness as he remembered how the day had begun. "That means a lot to me."

"As much as I'm starting to like you, Kyle, if this goes anywhere, it's going there for Teddy."

He nodded, understanding. It wasn't about what Kyle wanted or needed to be true, but what Teddy needed to be known.

It was then he saw Dylan in the hallway, looking at him. The two of them exchanged quick nods, as Dylan disappeared to the men's room and Kyle got up to follow.

"Be careful, Detective Callahan," she said.

No, Kyle realized, she didn't miss a thing.

"Isn't meeting in a bathroom a little . . . I don't know, B-movieish?"

Kyle was leaning against the wall while Dylan poked his head out the door a last time to make sure no one was coming.

Dylan bent down and looked under the stalls: no one there, the coast appeared to be clear.

"I can't risk being overheard," he said, in a voice so low and soft he assured he would not be.

"Dylan, listen –"

"I saw you with the cop lady. She shouldn't be here."

"You run a public establishment. Besides, she'll be a lesbian soon and she has to start somewhere."

"Can we not joke for the moment?" Dylan said, and Kyle realized he was truly afraid.

"What's going on here?"

"I don't know!" Dylan said, his voice rising. "I don't know! That's the problem. I think Sid stole the money to buy this place."

"I thought he inherited the money from an aunt."

"That's what he said, but why is it I never met this aunt? And when I went searching . . . nothing, Kyle. If there was a rich aunt he never mentioned until she left him all this money, she did a very good job of taking any trace of herself to the grave. Wherever that it. No, I think he stole the money, and I think Teddy found out."

"A fatal bit of information, so it seems."

"Please, I so much don't want to think that. We've been together for ten years. I know Sid, he wouldn't hurt anyone."

Kyle waited a moment, hoping Dylan would relax enough to have a conversation that wasn't infused with panic.

"So he wouldn't hurt anyone, but he would steal a million dollars, or whatever the Lodge cost . . ."

"Most of it's the land. And yes, I'm afraid he would. But I can't say for sure he did! He told me it was an inheritance."

"Good timing."

"Good timing, indeed. I never questioned him. There wasn't any reason to, and . . . no desire to. I mean, this was the chance of a lifetime, a dream come true."

"Where would he get his hands on that kind of money?" Kyle asked.

"He worked at a bank!" Dylan hissed, and it was suddenly clear. If Sid had stolen the money, he had embezzled it; a large sum of it, which could not go unnoticed, at least not forever.

"You need to speak to the police," Kyle said. "And they need to speak to the bank."

Dylan was crestfallen, his face expressing pain and indecision. This was his partner, his husband, the man he planned to spend the rest of his life with.

"I can't," he said.

Suddenly Kyle knew why they were having this conversation: Dylan wanted him to be the one to go to the authorities. He'd been able to reveal his suspicions to Kyle, but not to take it further, not to put his prints on a noose that might soon be around Sid Stanhope's neck.

"I have to tell her," Kyle said, meaning Detective Sikorsky. "I'm not in a position to do anything else with this information."

Dylan nodded, having accepted as much.

Kyle felt terribly for this man whom he could at best call an acquaintance. They'd never had a long conversation, never shared a meal, but he thought of what it would mean to him if Danny faced a crisis that could separate them. Danny, of course, would never commit a crime, let alone murder, but life had a way of dropping boulders on the unsuspecting.

"I don't know why I told you this," Dylan said, regretting his decision to speak to Kyle.

"Because you have a conscience," Kyle said, and he started to leave.

Dylan grabbed his arm. "He's not a killer. I don't know how Teddy ended up in the pool, but Sid didn't put him there. I refuse to believe that."

Kyle believed him – not that Sid was incapable of killing someone (a million-five was a serious motive), but that Dylan loved him enough to deny it. He patted Dylan's hand, gently removed it from his arm and headed back to the bar.

Pete was singing Billy Joel's "The Piano Man", joined in the chorus by a half dozen guests ringing the piano. Kyle walked back in and looked to the sofa, only to see it was empty. He wandered to the bar instead.

"She left with someone," Cowboy Dave said, knowing who Kyle was looking for.

So she wasn't such a novice after all, and while she may not have come there looking for a date, she'd had no trouble accepting one.

"That Bo chick," Dave said, as if Kyle must know who she was. His use of the word "chick" seemed dated and quaint, given that few women at Pride Lodge would consider themselves chicks.

It struck Kyle as odd; Bo had told Sid and the others at the table she would not be going to the bar later that night. He wondered if she'd simply had a change of heart, or if perhaps she hoped to get lucky. Rural Pennsylvania can be a lonely place at night, even at Pride Lodge.

Good for her, he thought, reflecting on the detective meeting up with the loner from St. Paul. Maybe fate would treat them well, at least for a weekend.

He waved goodnight at Dave and Pete, smiled at the enjoyment everyone was having at another Halloween weekend at Pride Lodge, and headed upstairs. As he came into the great room he saw old Jeremy in his chair, alone now, watching his Dracula movie in the dark.

"Good night, Jeremy," he said, crossing in front of the television.

"Good night, Detective Callahan," Jeremy replied, never taking his eyes off Christopher Lee.

It wasn't until Kyle was almost back to the room that he reflected on what a strange thing it was for Jeremy to say. As if he had been in the booth with Kyle and the detective when she called him the same thing. It's one thing not to miss a trick, another altogether not to miss one you never saw.

Chapter Nineteen

NATURAL CAUSES

Kyle was surprised to find Danny awake first on Saturday morning. He discovered it when he reached across the bed, half asleep, and found an empty mattress next to him. He looked up, focused, and saw Danny sitting at the small table with his restaurant notes and a reading flashlight.

"Why don't you turn the light on?" Kyle said, his voice thick with sleep.

"I didn't want to wake you," Danny said. He was wearing just his boxer shorts and t-shirt.

Kyle rolled back, facing the ceiling. "I thought you weren't going to work this weekend."

"I'm not working."

"So what's on your mind? You're never up at – " and he glanced at the clock on the nightstand – "six-thirty! On a weekend?"

Kyle remembered not getting back to the cabin until after midnight. "What's troubling you?" he said, knowing from his years with Danny that the only thing that would have him out of bed this early was worry.

"She's going to be eighty next week. That's old, you know."

Margaret Bowman was a second mother to Danny. She'd taken him under her wing and nurtured him along, and had hinted more than once to him that he was her heir apparent. With no children of her own, and no nieces or nephews who were interested in the business, even if she had been inclined to leave it to them, she had begun to think Margaret's Passion would die with her. Then along came Danny and it seemed fated that they would form the sort of mentor/parent bond they had. Danny was dreading his own parents' passing enough as it was; the thought of Margaret coming to the end of her years weighed on him.

"She's sharp as a tack," Kyle said. "And she still gets around very nicely. She comes down and talks to people in the restaurant. Why are you thinking about this?"

"I don't know. I just feel time passing, that's all." And then, suddenly, "We should get married, next year."

They'd talked about marriage ever since New York passed a bill making it legal. At first Kyle had wanted to make the trip to City Hall quickly, seeing the rush of excitement and the sight of history unfolding on television. He thought their fifth anniversary, which was only a month away then, would be an ideal time to get married. But the thrill quickly died down and both men decided to take an informed approach: what does marriage mean, what are the legal ramifications, what is the hurry? They knew they would do it, but they would do it in their own time. And now, unexpectedly, Danny was pushing to make it official: to be husbands in more than name only.

"Well," Kyle said, "a wedding takes time. It's October now – November, really – so maybe next summer . . ."

"Next year, for sure," Danny said. Then, glancing at the seating chart for Margaret's birthday luncheon, "I'm sure she'll make it another year. Hell, another ten. She's a tough old bird."

Kyle wasn't comfortable when Danny became melancholy. He knew Danny sometimes fell into a dark reverie about life without his parents, who were both in their late 70s, and the inevitability of losing Margaret. He even fretted every time they went to the vet that Smelly and Leonard were facing down Father Time as well. All of them were. Kyle just chose not to dwell on it. He picked up the television remote from the nightstand and turned on the TV, wanting to watch the news and change the subject.

There on the local channel was a young woman reporter, dressed warmly for the weather but still television-pretty with strawberry blonde hair and a face perfectly made up at six o'clock on a Saturday morning. Her breath was coming out in clouds, which told Kyle it was colder than it had been yesterday. Wetter, too, as it appeared to have been raining where the woman was. Identified on the screen as Ellie Cameron from Philly6, she stood in a wooded area while several policemen moved around behind her.

"The body found in Chester Creek has been identified as Happy Corcoran."

"What?!" Kyle shouted, sitting up in bed.

"A neighbor of Mr. Corcoran's from Stockton, New Jersey, responded to our earlier report on a body found in the woods and called authorities. Apparently Mr. Corcoran has been missing for several days and the neighbor thought the description was familiar. The coroner is declining comment on a cause of death until an autopsy's been performed. As you can see, police continue to search the area for evidence of just what happened here, and when. If you have any information about Happy Corcoran and his movements, please contact them immediately. All calls are kept confidential. This is Ellie Cameron from Philly6, back to you, Carlton."

Kyle hit the mute button. He and Danny both stared at the television, stunned.

"That reporter's a long way from Philly," Danny said. "I think. I mean, where the hell is Chester Creek?"

"Far enough from civilization that a body could lie there for days without anyone seeing it. And a body in a creek is news for a local Philadelphia station. It's only an hour from here."

"This isn't going to go well," Danny said, and Kyle knew he meant at the Lodge. "We can't be the only people who saw this. Poor Cowboy Dave. They had a thing, you know. Before Happy and Teddy. Or maybe at the same time, kids are like that."

"I didn't know, but I guessed. The way Dave talked about him. So sad. And so mysterious. I mean, think about it. Happy goes missing three days ago. Teddy dies at the bottom of the pool yesterday."

"Do you want to check out?" Danny said. "Go back to the City?"

Kyle looked at him, surprised. "God no, not now. I want to know what's going on here. I want to talk to Detective Sikorsky." He swung his legs around and sat up on the edge of the bed. He was wearing the red plaid pajama bottoms he always slept up. He slid his feet into the slippers Danny had given him. "And I want to do some research. Something about the exchange at dinner between Sid and that Bo woman, it was odd. And she said she wasn't going to the bar last night but did, and left with the detective! I don't know, I'm just curious. Please tell me you brought the laptop, I haven't seen it out."

"It's in the suitcase," Danny said. "Have I ever forgotten it?"

"Yes, in Key West."

"And you'll never let me forget it. All those amazing photographs that had to wait for you to post on your blog until we got home. Consider it a lesson in patience."

Kyle got out of bed and walked over to the suitcase. He wanted his morning coffee and some time with a search engine.

"You want the sound back on?" he asked.

"Leave it off," Danny said, sliding his papers to the side. "We've had enough excitement for now, and a lot more waiting up the hill."

Chapter Twenty

ROOM 202

*T*he moon was so large the sight of it took Bo's breath away as she glanced across the bed, out past the window into the night sky. The blackness of the heavens in the Pennsylvania countryside had struck her the first night here; before that, even, as she'd driven from St. Paul, along back roads, far away from city lights that stole the majesty of the stars. They were bare and innumerable here. She likened them to the beauty of the woman lying next to her, breathing gently in her sleep. She chose to ignore the irony of sleeping next to the very woman whose choices in life were her polar opposite: Linda Sikorsky, detective, seeker of facts, if not truth, justice personified as she followed and tracked and peered into puzzles, with her one goal of solving them and stopping even that small evil in the world. Bo Sweetzer, Emily Lapinsky as a child, a good person from all appearances, a woman set on revenge behind the goodness. She didn't fool herself; while many people would say the men she'd killed had only got what they deserved, she knew in a society reliant on law and order that she, too, was a murderer. There were no degrees of murder and those who commit it: killing was killing, and here she was, a killer, watching someone she could so easily love, asleep and dreaming beside her, who would not hesitate to see her sentenced to a life behind bars.

What was an assassin to do? Should she slip away now, so soon after first light? Should she abandon her mission, let the old man live, and try to build a life *with this policewoman? A life of secrets and lies? Or should she – and this she knew to be the answer – complete the one true objective of her life: to silence the voices that had haunted her for thirty years, to put an end to the screams of a child watching her parents be coldly, brutally murdered. For a handful of cash. A television set. A watch. She sighed, knowing what she had to do, that she would be taking one life while setting free another, and that after the coming day she would never see this woman again, this woman whose shoulders she now leaned over gently and caressed.*

Bo rolled over in her empty bed and stared out the window, seeing it would be a sunny day. The clouds had moved on and left in their place a startling blue sky. She let the fantasy go, let it evaporate like morning dew, and was both amused and troubled by her willingness to think the unthinkable. Nothing had happened between them except in her imagination. It was just as well, since her imagination had always been a dark and lonely place. Only the men she exacted revenge upon belonged there.

They had had coffee and pie at the Eagle Diner in New Hope. Bo admitted to herself she had wanted more – expected more, in the way we sometimes allow ourselves to think we are entitled to something simply because we wish it – but Sikorsky had not promised anything at all, spoken or unspoken, and she had not led Bo to believe their trip away from the Lodge was anything other than a friendly ride to a nearby diner for a private chat. That was something almost charming about people unsure of their own sexuality: they often didn't realize there might be something suggestive in simply asking someone out for coffee. By the time they'd finished, however, Bo wasn't so sure the detective was just curious, or that she hadn't meant to send signals.

It had started simply enough: Bo had been unable to sleep. After two hours of lying in bed in a dark room, staring at the ceiling, she decided to head to the piano bar and have something to drink. Non-alcoholic, since she seldom drank and had committed not to while she carried out her mission. But anything would help, and she'd hoped that being in the bar would distract her mind enough that after a while she could return to her room and sleep.

She had never been a bar-goer. Bars unsettled her. They upended her sense of the world as essentially a lonely place where even two people who shared a life remained strangers in some ways. Quiet ways. Ways never spoken of, for saying them out loud might peel away the illusions so central to love and companionship. Bo had loved only once, and that, she'd come to know, was a mistake. As for companionship, it was dangerous. Even someone as tightly controlled as she was could let something slip; it was much better never to court error. But there she was, sitting on a stool at the Lodge's bar, watching as some guests chatted and mingled in costumes, others in their street clothes. She recognized the lesbian couple Eileen and Maggie. Eileen didn't notice her, and Maggie was busy once again reading something on her cell phone. The man Danny had so disliked – Lionel? Linus? – continued to hold court, this time around a small table with the two disciples who'd been at each arm since he arrived. The young boy-toy was nowhere in sight.

She was halfway through her Ginger Ale when she felt someone come up behind her. She didn't believe in a sixth-sense, but that we feel shifts in the air, or we manage to connect very distant dots and determine their destination point before they get there. Mysterious, yes, but not inexplicable. She just knew someone was behind her, and she swiveled around on her bar-stool. Much to her surprise she found Detective Linda Sikorsky not more than two feet away, as startled to have Bo turn around just then as Bo was to see her there. She was wearing jeans and a blouse, Bo noticed, looking much less like a cop and much more like the kind of women she imagined sought one another out in the bars she did not go to.

"Hello, Ms. Sweetzer," the detective said. She didn't extend her hand, and already Bo could tell she was nervous, unsure if a handshake was called for or if withholding it would be rude.

"I prefer 'Miss,' actually," Bo said. "I've never been a missus and the whole 'Ms' thing is too much of an artifice for me. Call me old-school."

Linda smiled, and Bo couldn't tell if she was amused or pleased; possibly both.

"Well, then, Miss Sweetzer, how are you enjoying your evening? Have you been here before?"

Bo was suddenly suspicious. She'd told the detective in their morning interview that she had never been to Pride Lodge before. She wondered if the approach was just part of the job, or if Linda Sikorsky was trying to trip her up for some reason.

"Oh, wait, you told me that," Linda said, shaking her head at her own forgetfulness. "Even cops forget things."

And she's a mind-reader, too, Bo thought. I like this woman.

"I tried to go to sleep," Bo said. "I'm not really a party person, or a bar person, but I am an insomniac on occasion. This was one of those occasions. I figured a drink might settle my mind down."

Linda looked at the half-empty glass on the counter in front of Bo. "May I get you another?" she asked.

"It's only soda. Not the sort of thing that makes you want more."

There was a moment of silence that quickly grew awkward, and Bo realized that Linda wasn't very skilled in these situations. Chasing down criminals she could do very well, but striking up and maintaining a conversation with another woman in a gay bar? Not so used to that.

"How about some coffee?" Linda said.

Bo burst out laughing.

"What? What did I say?"

"You just asked an insomniac if she'd like a cup of coffee."

"And I forgot you'd never been here," Linda said, embarrassed. "Strike two. But maybe I meant decaf. Yes! I meant decaf! And a piece of pie . . . unless sugar keeps you up, too."

Bo thought about it a moment.

"Not here," Linda said. "The kitchen's closed down anyway. But there's a restaurant not far from here, the Eagle Diner. Twenty-four hour place. It'd give you a chance to see a little more of the area."

"In the dark."

"Well, yeah. But that's not a bad way to see it. We could come across some deer in the headlights."

Bo wondered who was the deer, and who was the headlights. Sikorsky was clearly a very intelligent woman, and she might yet have questions in mind to ask Bo that Bo would not answer, at least not truthfully. But she couldn't sleep, and she found the detective attractive, and she was very skilled at only revealing what she wanted people to see. So why not?

"Let's go," Bo said, sliding off the stool. "I can't think of anywhere I'd rather end the night than at the Eagle Diner. Unless that's not where it ends."

She saw the sudden flush in Linda's face: Bo had her number, and the detective knew it. "Relax," she said. "I was just having some fun. Now let's go get that pie! They have ice cream there?"

"It's a diner," Linda said. "Of course they do."

The two women headed out of the bar. Cowboy Dave watched them go and smiled: another romance blossoming at Pride Lodge. He'd seen more than a few.

The Eagle Diner was on Highway 202, a stone's throw from the Giant grocery store and just up the road from the Raven, a gay hotel, restaurant and gathering place that had been there for decades, with the occasional interruption. They knew each other, of course, the Raven and Pride Lodge, and had remained friendly as long they'd both been in business. Pride Lodge was more out of the way, and people who stayed there tended not to be the same customers who would stay at the Raven. There had never been any real rivalry between the two: there were enough gay, lesbian, bisexual and transgender patrons to keep them both operating this long. Throw in the Q's, I's, and any letters not yet added to the acronym, and business should stay brisk for years to come.

Bo's suspicions that Linda Sikorsky was somehow on to her vanished quickly enough once they were seated in a booth. The diner had quite a few customers even this close to midnight, and the two women did not stand out in any way. They'd each ordered apple pie and coffee (Bo had started to suggest one pie, two forks, but thought better of it) and were several bites in when Sikorsky made her motives known.

"I've lived in this area all my life," she said, glancing around nervously to make sure no one was eavesdropping. She was well-known enough in New Hope that she had to always be aware someone might recognize her. "I'm thirty-six years old. Everybody knows me."

"And everybody thinks you're a lesbian," Bo said.

Linda stared at her, taken aback. While she wasn't going to state it that way – unsure exactly how she would state it – that's what she was thinking and trying to articulate.

"But you're not," Bo continued. "Or you're not sure, and what better way to crystallize it for yourself than ask a real one out for coffee and advice."

"You're either a cop," said Linda, laughing nervously, "or a psychic." She paused a moment. "I don't suppose you're wondering, why you."

"I know why me. Because I'm cute! Shorter than you, about the right age, Minnesota nice, and, from your own notes, I'm sure, single."

"I've never dated a woman," Linda said. "I've thought about it. My father's dead and my mother lives alone in Philly. It's not like I have to worry what they'll think of me. And my only sibling is a brother who lives in New York City with a man twenty years older than him that he calls his benefactor. Who the hell cares if I'm a lesbian? Which I'm not saying I am, since it's hard to say when you've never done anything but imagine it."

"Well," said Bo gently, "you're free to imagine it all you want to with me. I won't ask you to act on it." And she winked. "Not tonight."

Linda visibly relaxed. She had fantasized for years having this conversation with someone, but she had honestly never thought the right time – or the right woman – would come. If she were simply blunt with herself she would say yes, Linda, you're attracted to women, and that pretty much makes you a lesbian, but she had not been honest. She had clung to uncertainty as a way of avoiding having to come clean: to her friends, who probably already knew, to her neighbors, and to her colleagues – the people she dreaded telling most. It was a small force, and she knew, she truly knew, they would think just as highly of her after she came out as they had the moment before, and that they would probably start trying to line her up with dates. Marriage was a reality for same-sex couples these days, even if they had to travel out of state to do it, and knowing the people she worked with every day, a few of them would expect to be invited to her wedding, the sooner the better.

"You're here until when?" Linda asked. "Just in case I have a few more questions about the investigation, of course."

"Of course," Bo said. "I'm set to check out Sunday, but who knows, I kind of like the place, I might want to stay a few days and see more. If it's got an Eagle Diner, I can only imagine what else is going on here."

The two women laughed. Bo felt her heart sink, suddenly, painfully conscious of the lie she'd told and what it meant. She would never see Linda Sikorsky again after tonight. She intended to see her mission through to its deadly conclusion and be gone well before Sunday's first light flooded the sky. Unless . . .

"Are you coming to the party tomorrow?" Bo asked. "The Halloween party?"

"I wasn't planning on it," Linda replied, and she waved at the waitress for the check. "But now I'm thinking maybe. I don't have a costume."

"Come as Cupid," Bo said, smiling. "It's a natural fit."

Bo wondered why she was doing this to herself, asking a woman she clearly desired to come back the next night, the night she planned to claim her final revenge and go. You're slipping, Bo, she told herself, all the while smiling as Dottie, the waitress, left the check on the table between them. Maybe you don't have the heart for it, maybe you want a happy ending after all. She felt a sting in her eyes – an unfamiliar fall for a woman who had not cried in thirty years, and she quickly looked away. It wouldn't matter if the cop came, it wouldn't matter how she felt about Bo or how she made Bo feel. The die had been cast in that bedroom three decades ago, and there was only one roll left. So let her come, let her think Bo had made a fool of her as she vanished in the night, let her never know the truth and how high its price.

Linda slid out of the booth and started to reach for Bo's hand. She happened to look over and see and old straight couple she had known for years, used her hand to wave to them instead, and led the way out.

Chapter Twenty-One

THE PAST CATCHES UP

Kyle hit a dead end in his internet searching. He'd been unable to find anything about Sid Stanhope until he ran across a group picture from a bank office in Newark. It was Sid alright, fifteen years younger but identifiable. And years later the items about Pride Lodge. Kyle realized Sid was not the type to spend much time online. He doubted he was on Facebook and he probably thought tweeting was something baby birds did when they were hungry. He had hit a dead end until he started thinking again about the odd, tense exchange between Sid and Bo at the restaurant. Maybe he was looking in the wrong direction, for the wrong person. Maybe she was a better lead to follow. Letting his hunch take him where it may, he started looking into Bo Sweetzer. BoAndBehold, pleasant jewelry designer from St. Paul. Ten minutes into his search he found the same article Sid had found and his breath stopped. Bo Sweetzer was not who she had always been. Once upon a time she'd been a young child named Emily Lapinsky, living far from St. Paul.

Kyle's pulse accelerated as he jumped from one link to the next, one dot to the next, connecting them at digital speed. He was reading what little he could find from so long ago when up popped a website called *DeathWatchLA*. At first glance it appeared to just be lurid, tabloid fodder:

morgue photos of dead celebrities, macabre stories of people murdered in sudden, gruesome acts of violence. It wasn't until he read the "about" section and saw that there had been a print predecessor, that in fact the website was based on a cheaply produced throwaway newspaper that hadn't been much more than a flyer in the 1980s, and that there were scanned PDF copies of the old issues available for $4.99 each (PayPal or credit card accepted), that he knew he might be onto something. He quickly got his Visa and randomly selected a dozen old issues, dating back to 1980. He was halfway through them, having read six without finding anything that struck him, when he came upon the Lapinsky murders. A burglary gone horribly wrong, involving a trio of thieves. The Los Feliz Gang, as the media dubbed them. Three men, a dead husband and wife, and a daughter who had escaped execution by hiding in the closet. There was a photo showing her in a Catholic school girl's uniform.

Kyle stared at her.

"Look at this," he said to Danny. Danny had been resting in bed reading an old New York Post he'd brought with them. Kyle never understood why Danny liked reading that paper, given its politics, but he knew it was a guilty pleasure, like watching a reality TV show that wasn't real in any way and that made the human race seem doomed.

Danny got out of bed and walked over to the table where Kyle was sitting with the laptop. He peered at the old photograph. "It's a girl," he said.

"Well, yeah, but does she remind you of anyone?"

"I can't say she does, sorry."

"Look closer."

Danny leaned down and peered at the photograph.

"Oh my God."

"Yes," Kyle said. "Our table mate from St. Paul." He slid the laptop away and started to pace. "I need to get into that room."

"Her room?"

"No, Teddy's. I need something solid to take to Sikorsky."

"Isn't this enough?" Danny asked, nodding at the article on the laptop.

"No, it's not. But I think there's something to be found . . . and I think Teddy found it. Maybe Happy, too. Or Teddy told him, or something like that. Their deaths are connected, I'm certain of that. And if we trace the line back, back, we can trace it all the way back to a house in Los Angeles thirty years ago."

"You should call Sikorsky now," Danny said. "This is dangerous territory. You could get hurt, Kyle."

"I won't get hurt. And I will talk to her, soon. Dylan will help me, he's already panicking over these suspicions he has. He'll let me in Teddy's room and I'll find something there, I'm sure of it. Then I call the police."

"You have to promise me."

"I promise," Kyle said. "Cross my heart . . ."

"Don't finish that! Nobody hopes to die, it's an awful expression. You know, Kyle, life is so much simpler when you just take pictures."

Kyle stopped pacing and shut the laptop. "Let's go have breakfast," he said. "I hear murder's on the menu."

Chapter Twenty-Two

BREAKFAST AT EPIPHANY'S

Most of the dozen or so people having breakfast didn't know who Happy was and hadn't heard about his death. Unlike many of the staff, he'd only been around a few months and seemed to have made the biggest impression on the two men he had dated, Teddy and Cowboy Dave. The other staff, on the other hand, had clearly gotten the news, and it made for a strange emotional mix: guests chatting about their plans for the day and wondering if the good weather would hold out, while Ricki manned the desk with a dazed expression on his face and Elzbetta, on table duty, only spoke when spoken to as she took their orders. Dylan, meanwhile, was visibly pale, with a fear in his eyes that couldn't be hidden by his wooden smile.

Kyle and Danny showed themselves to a table by the window overlooking the road.

"No camera this morning?" Danny asked, used to seeing Kyle with his Nikon slung around his neck. "It looks like a good day for photographs."

"I may need to move quickly," Kyle said, his voice low. "I can't worry about leaving a camera sitting around or having it swinging on my neck."

Just then Elzbetta came up to them. She was more sullen than usual, and appeared to have been crying.

"You heard about Happy," she said, posing it as a statement, as if everyone must have heard.

"We saw the news, yes," Kyle said.

"We were . . . friends."

"I'm sorry."

"We were going to go away, to the Rocky Mountains," she said. "Denver. He had family there."

Kyle and Danny exchanged glances: apparently there weren't many people young Happy did not sleep with.

"He didn't kill himself!" she blurted out.

Danny was startled. "Who said . . ."

"They speculated, the news guy I saw, he said they hadn't ruled out suicide, which means they've ruled it in!"

"Reporters don't know much," Kyle said, trying to reassure the distressed waitress. "That's why they're reporters."

"It's just fucked up. Seriously fucked up, like everything around here. This place is cursed, I can't stay. What did you want for breakfast?"

They placed their orders and were relieved to have Elzbetta finally walk away without saying anything more.

"Do you believe her?" Danny asked. "That Pride Lodge is cursed?"

"Don't be stupid," Kyle said, immediately regretting his use of a word Danny hated. Danny was not stupid by any definition, but somewhere in his life, probably his childhood, the word had been used to great effect against him. He glared at Kyle.

"I'm sorry," Kyle said. "I just meant it's preposterous. The Lodge has been a going concern for, what, almost thirty years, and suddenly it's cursed?"

"Stu died from a heart attack on those steps right there," Danny said, nodding toward the steps that led down the hill. "Not to mention the first owner's wife and children. Curses have to start somewhere."

"In our fevered imaginations, that's where."

Their conversation was interrupted as Bo Sweetzer came walking through the dining room and approached their table. They'd formed their own small group the last two days and it seemed natural to her to invite herself to join them. Kyle looked behind her, noticing she was alone.

"Looking for someone?" she said, smiling. She knew her departure the night before with the beautifully sturdy detective had not gone unnoticed.

Kyle blushed at his own transparency. "I thought you might be dining with someone else this morning."

"Dining," she said. "I like that. You don't usually think of people dining at breakfast."

Bo was in very good spirits. She either hadn't heard the news about poor Happy, or, more likely, she had no idea who he was. Most people relegated the deaths of strangers to the general news feed of their day.

"We only had coffee and dessert," she said, quelling Kyle's curiosity.

Danny hadn't been all that interested to begin with and was hoping their food would arrive soon. He reached for his water glass.

"She's questioning," Bo continued.

"And a sucker for a California girl, I'm guessing," Kyle said.

Danny nearly choked on his water.

"Oh, I'm sorry," Kyle corrected himself. "You're from Minnesota. St. Paul. My mistake."

The smile on Bo's face remained, but took on a rigid quality, as if it wanted to fall but she was keeping it in place by force of will. "It must have been the accent," she said, knowing there was no such thing as a California accent. "I did live there for a few years, when I was a child."

Danny carefully watched the two of them, worried that Kyle had tipped his hand too readily.

"We've been there a few times, haven't we, Danny?"

Danny nodded, hoping the subject would change.

"We stayed with friends in the Los Feliz area. Did you live anywhere near there?"

And now she knew. Kyle had all but told her who he thought she was. Unfortunately for him, she was close to her endgame and losing her need for concealment with each passing hour. She had come to believe, since her time with Detective Sikorsky the night before, that while she would see an end to her mission, her mission would also be the end of her. If she made it away from Pride Lodge, having fulfilled the promise she had repeated to her parents' ghosts for thirty years, she would have to abandon Bo Sweetzer as completely and easily as she had abandoned Emily Lapinsky. Sid Stanhope was not the last person she would kill after all.

"Oddly enough," she said, the smile now gone, "that's one of the few neighborhoods I never saw. We were on the west side, not far from Century City. I was just a kid, I don't even remember the name of where we lived."

"Have you gone back?" Kyle asked.

"No, I've never had the interest," she said, and Kyle could see a sadness come over her. She suddenly struck him as very old, and very tired, a woman coming to the end of her journey, whatever that journey might be.

"Does anybody care that Happy's gone?" Elzbetta said, coming up to their table carrying plates with their breakfast. "It doesn't seem to me anybody gives a shit."

"Who's Happy?" Bo asked. "What happened?"

While Elzbetta gave a quick rundown on who Happy was and that he'd been found dead in a creek the night before, Kyle looked over to see Dylan signaling him, nodding toward the kitchen.

"Excuse me," Kyle said, standing and putting his napkin on his chair. "I need to wash my hands."

Kyle left the table and headed toward the restrooms. When he got to the hallway that led back to them, he veered left into the kitchen and saw Dylan standing there with an apron on.

"Cece called in sick. She's our morning cook," he said. "When you run a place like this you have to know how to do everything."

Dylan wiped his hands on his apron and began to pace. "Happy's dead, before Teddy, from what they said on the news. Do you think Teddy knew?"

"I think Teddy knew too many things," Kyle said. "That's why I need to get into his room."

"Do you think he did it?" Dylan asked.

"What, kill Happy?"

"No!"

And with that Kyle knew he meant Sid. It struck him how quickly Dylan had allowed himself to believe Sid could be a thief, and now a murderer.

"I wouldn't read too much into the timing of this," Kyle said, trying to calm the situation. "Happy left days ago."

"Yes, and he didn't say anything to anyone about it, and he turned up dead in a creek. Before or after Teddy died at the bottom of the pool, we won't know until they announce it. Maybe Happy died last night, maybe he died the day he disappeared! Can you imagine being dead in the woods for three days? Oh my God, the animals. Unless his body was moved!"

"Listen, Dylan," Kyle said, "I need to get into Teddy's room. It's not sealed off. There isn't any crime scene at this point, as far as the police are concerned. You can be there, I'll be very respectful, but I have to have something solid to show Sikorsky. So far it's all just crazy imaginings, however un-crazy they are to you and me."

"I want to wait until Sid's not around," Dylan said, nodding. "He'll know something's up if we go in Teddy's room."

"Just tell him I want something to remember Teddy by."

"He's a very smart man, he'll know better. No, let's wait."

Kyle would normally not go looking through someone's belongings, let alone a dead man's, but he was convinced a significant piece of the puzzle might well be in Teddy's room.

"Sid's going into New Hope this afternoon," Dylan said. "For more party supplies. We'll have plenty of locals coming tonight, we always run out of something. That's the time for this, when he's safely away for a few hours."

"Perfect," Kyle said. "Text me when it's time, we'll be in the cabin. And now I think I'll get back out there. You wait a minute so it's not too obvious we're having an affair."

Dylan smiled for the first time that day and watched as Kyle went back to the table.

Chapter Twenty-Three

A LATE START

etective Linda Sikorsky. Even after fifteen years on the force, three of them as the only active homicide detective in New Hope (a job she performed for other towns in the area when needed, so seldom did murders occur in this bucolic stretch of Pennsylvania), Linda still felt uncomfortable with the title. As if she'd come to it by accident, or been given the position when someone else had displayed more merit for it. But there was no one else, and she had worked long and hard to get where she was. It just seemed like such a dream come true, regardless of how few people dream of being homicide detectives. It wasn't the sort of thing you'd hear from little girls asked what they wanted to be when they grew up. A nurse, maybe, or a teacher, or a pop star, but not someone whose job it was to investigate the killing of one human being by another. Still, it had been her dream ever since she'd been a child in Cincinnati and her father, a cop on the Cincinnati Police Department, was gunned down in the most absurd way: as a bystander when shots broke out during a fight outside a grocery store. A grocery store! Not a bar, not a craps game he was breaking up, not anything that said "hero" when the papers covered the story the next day. Oh, they called him a hero. Every person in uniform was instantly transformed into a hero when they died, even if it was from a heart attack in a church parking lot. But try as she did, she was never able to think of her father's death as the death of a hero. It was a cruel, capricious, meaningless death, when he had stopped at the store to pick up a short list of groceries her mother had given him over the phone, and as he was walking to his car in the parking lot, two thugs started shouting at each other outside the main entrance. By the time Peter Sikorsky was even aware that trouble was happening, a bullet had entered his skull on the right side, just about the temple, and taken a sizable chunk of his head with it on the way out.

It had never made sense to her, and she had long ago stopped trying to make it. Ideas like "closure" and making sense of random tragedy were for people more desperate to believe everything happened for a reason. She knew better. She knew people were felled by stray bullets and children were raped and very few people were heroes. But while she would not humor others by calling her father's death anything but senseless, she would honor him by becoming a police officer and seeking out a career he had been deprived of. That was thirty-five years ago, in a world and life so removed from the one she now lived that she only believed it had ever happened because it had happened to her. Her mother, Estelle Sikorsky, had met another man two years after her father's death, and the three of them had moved to Philadelphia. Her stepfather, too, had died, but from a stroke, something less dramatic but no less sudden or pointless, and her mother now lived alone six blocks from Independence Hall. She recently retired from her job teaching fifth and sixth graders, and Linda visited her once a month, making the hour's drive to sit and talk about this and that, never anything too deep, including the men who had died on Estelle and left her sitting alone in her kitchen on Sunday afternoons.

That they never spoke of anything too sensitive was a big reason Linda had never told her mother, or anyone else, that she was – all things being considered – a lesbian. Linda didn't like calling herself anything. And, at the same time, she was very honest and always had been. Someone who could not kid herself about the brutal and meaningless nature of her father's death could not kid herself about her own nature. She had known she was attracted to women long before she was one herself. Back when she was a child, in middle school, probably earlier. But she had chosen, for reasons she still did not fully understand, to never label it, to never call herself any-thing other than Linda. She had chosen as well not to act on it. Not because she was ashamed, or wanted to be something other than who she was, but because she feared the loss it could bring. That, she had finally come to realize, was the real reason: not any perceived hostility, not some sad self-rejection, but because a bullet had taken away the one man she had loved in her life, and she feared, in a way words could not express and consciousness could not quite define, that acting on her desires would open the door to love, and love would open the door to loss.

Even last night, when she had asked Bo out and they'd had coffee at the diner, she felt herself as much repelled as attracted, as if something were in front of her that she both wanted and feared. Something that simultane-ously promised pleasure and threatened pain – comfort with a caveat. It had been her way of testing waters whose shore she had stood gazing from for twenty years. It had not been a particular attraction to Bo Sweetzer, but a way of finally saying, yes, this is me, this is who I am and who I want to be. She was grateful to have made this initial foray into her truest identity with someone as nice, patient and free from expectation as the woman from St. Paul. That this woman, Linda now knew, was not who she pretended to be complicated things but did not take away the simple joy she'd had the night before, sitting in a diner with another woman, for all to see (most of whom, she knew, had assumed she was gay all this time anyway). It had given her a sense of freedom she had always hoped was available but was never really sure, until then, until that moment when she went from ques-tioning to certainty. That was hers to keep, despite what came of the things she'd learned after going home and, instead of sleeping, doing what an obsessive detective does: investigating. Bo Sweetzer, jewelry maker, web-site, history, dead end. And if there was one thing Linda Sikorksy did not like, it was a dead end. There were already too many at Pride Lodge for comfort.

In this day of social networks, data mining and seemingly endless pub-lic access to anyone who has ever typed their name online, it's a major accomplishment to have nothing about yourself available to anyone with a keyboard. The jewelry site was easy enough to find, its whole purpose was to sell jewelry and Bo gave the URL to everyone she met. But when Linda tried to dig a little deeper, find a college record, a past, it stopped. Bo Sweetzer had told her in their initial interview she was from St. Paul. Apparently that was truer than Linda could imagine: there was no Bo Sweetzer before St. Paul. Bo had managed to emerge fully formed from the world's womb, if not her mother's. And while it wasn't all that miraculous for her to remain off Facebook and Twitter and the other hubs of virtual friendship, followers and fanatics, it was nearly astonishing to simply arrive online as a twenty year old.

Linda had not spent the entire night trying to solve a puzzle she had created for herself. She was too tired, and, to be honest, not that concerned with what she had found – or not found – about a woman she would never see again after this weekend. But she made a note to herself to ask Bo about this at the Halloween party that night. She had decided to go, even though it meant pulling together some kind of costume at the last minute. All the years she'd been in New Hope and she had never spent an hour at Pride Lodge. Maybe she'd been avoiding it, maybe it offered answers to questions she had not been fully prepared to ask until last night. But here she was, planning to spend yet more of her weekend there. And not all for fun . . . the questions had changed, and the answers could be fatal. She would need to be prepared.

Chapter Twenty-Four

ON THE ROPES

Sid didn't know what was happening, only that something terrible was coming his way and leaving dead men in its tracks. First Frank and Sam, then Teddy, and now Happy. It was a trail, he had no doubt about that, and it led to him. Time was not on his side; he would need to make his escape soon. The Halloween party that night seemed like a perfect opportunity, when everyone was distracted, having a good time, drinking too much. No one would notice him driving away, and if they did, they would never dream he would not be back.

At first he'd thought what everyone else did, that Teddy had fallen into the pool. He had claimed to be sober for several months, but Sid had known a drunk or two in his life and as lovable as they may be, they could not be trusted to tell the truth when it came to their drinking. So he had assumed Teddy had relapsed, "slipped" they called it, and had somehow fallen into the empty pool. But the martini glass was odd. Sid had always seen Teddy with a tumbler of whiskey, never something so sophisticated as a martini. But he also knew that an alcoholic wasn't generally choosy, and it may have been that Teddy took whatever was at hand. Or at least that's what Sid had believed, had wanted to believe, until Happy. Too many deaths in too short a time, with the real possibility his own would be next.

Sid had spent the last twenty-four hours trying to put the pieces together and only getting more confused with each attempt. If the Bo woman was behind this, which seemed a conclusion impossible not to draw, why would she kill Teddy? Why Happy? She would have had to be here days ago, staying somewhere else. Or, as he had begun to fear, was more than one person involved, perhaps even conspiring to pull the noose ever tighter around his neck? Had Teddy found out that Sid Stanhope had been in the Lapinsky house that night thirty years ago? Was he planning to go to the police? That would certainly throw a wrench into the killer's plans; taking down the last of them would be impossible if Sid was behind bars. It seemed ever more likely that Teddy had unknowingly put himself in harm's way, directly in the path of someone who had no hesitation leaving dead bodies behind her. But why Happy? And why now?

The now of it was as mysterious as anything to Sid, maybe the most mysterious. They'd gotten away with it for three decades. They had all moved on, two of them leaving Los Angeles, with nothing to tie them together . . . except a watch. Sid had told himself all these years that he was innocent, really, in the scheme of things. He had never hurt anyone, had never even carried a gun. He was expecting the same thing they'd experienced at all the other houses: a quick in and out, no one home, no harm done, but then the Lapinksys had been there, and Frank, oh Frank . . .

Sid felt his eyes watering and immediately took control of his emotions. He would have to leave Dylan, and do it without saying why. No one could know what became of him or why he disappeared. He loved Dylan and had counted on spending his last years with him, years that would require companionship as his body found itself more and more worn down. Their age difference would put Dylan in the position of taking care of Sid, but they both knew that and Dylan even joked about it from time to time. It was not, he had said over and over, something he would consider a burden, but an honor, a continued demonstration of his love for Sid. And for this he would be betrayed, abandoned, left wondering for the rest of his life what had happened.

It was for Dylan's own good, Sid told himself. Anyone who would murder someone as hapless and accidental as Teddy Pembroke would not hesitate to turn their sights on Dylan if he was seen to be a threat. The sooner and cleaner Sid made his break, the better for them all.

He got up from his computer where he'd been looking at maps and reading about places where a man could disappear easily enough; not all of them were big cities, either. There are many small towns, not much more than bumps in the road, where there are few people to ask questions and vast spaces into which a man can disappear. He erased his search history and tried to focus on a plan. He was heading soon into New Hope for more supplies for that night. He would fill up the gas tank when he was there and buy some supplies of a more personal nature, food stuffs and water, packing for a long journey whose end he would only know when he got there. And then, sometime that night, when everyone was having a good time and looking the other way, Sid Stanhope would simply go away.

Chapter Twenty-Five

CABIN 6

Kyle was sitting cross-legged on the bed, the laptop open in front of him. Next to the laptop was his camera, with a USB cable running from it to the laptop: Kyle had downloaded all the photographs he'd taken since they arrived. He had come to believe over the years of taking pictures that people experience the world in images, one instant after another in a series that stretched from birth to death, and that, without intending it, answers could be found among the many accidental photographs he took. It was why he wore the Nikon around his neck nearly everywhere he went. He seldom knew what he would shoot, or, looking back over the forty or fifty pictures he might take in a day, what he would find.

"What are you looking for this time?" Danny asked. He was wearing beige shorts and a sweatshirt, settling in to rest until dinner and the party. The weather hadn't turned especially bad, but the sky had filled with clouds and a chilly rain looked likely. He had no desire to go sightseeing or make a trip into town. For Danny, the weekends at Pride Lodge were about resting, about not looking at seating charts (even though he did peek), about lying in bed reading a newspaper with the television turned low in the background. He knew Kyle was looking for answers in his photographs, but that was his process for making order of chaos, of connecting dots that otherwise formed no pattern.

"I don't know, you know that. That's the point. I'll know what I'm looking for when I see it."

"Are you calling Imogene back?" Danny asked. Kyle's boss had been trying to reach him since early that morning, but Kyle had successfully ignored her voicemails and texts. Danny wondered if he had finally convinced Kyle that he was not on call for Imogene twenty-four hours a day.

"It's just withdrawals," Kyle said absently, peering intently at his laptop screen. "She has to go cold turkey. Forty-eight hours from now and I'll be back, handing her a cheese Danish and a cup of coffee from Cecil's and it'll be like I was never away."

Cecil's was a diner on 46th Street near the studios where Japan TV3 rented space for their programming. Kyle happened upon it the first day they were working there and had presented Imogene with of cup of their rich, distinctive coffee most mornings since then.

"You're making progress," Danny said.

"You forget there's been a murder," Kyle said, reminding Danny of the one thing that could take his attention away so completely; unfortunately, it also reminded Danny that he was not that thing, that only the puzzle of death by suspicious circumstances was enough to get Kyle to let Imogene go to voicemail. It had happened the year before, when they had gone on a cruise to Canada and a woman was found dead in one of the steam rooms at the ship's very pricey spa. Sudden and unexplained, they'd said, but surely natural. A stroke, or a heart attack, perhaps an aneurism. Kyle had seen the woman being intimate with a man who was not her husband, and when the authorities thanked him for his information, clearly intending to ignore it, he had spent the rest of the cruise proving the cause of death was most unnatural. For that he had been thanked a second time, though no more sincerely, and never been credited for bringing the woman's husband to justice. Now here they were, in their own territory, so to speak, with friends and acquaintances at their favorite resort – a gay resort, where one would expect to find nothing more exciting than a drunken argument or a fling gone wrong – and Kyle was lost in thought again, trying to find connections.

The luck of the lens did not appear to be with him this time. Nothing in the dozens of photographs he had taken since they arrived told him anything. He didn't even know what he was looking for, some image that would tell him what words could not. It had been a picture of the woman on the cruise ship kissing her paramour by the hanging lifeboats, taken accidentally when Kyle was aiming for a shot of the walkway, that gave him the evidence he needed in the cruise ship murder. But so far this weekend at Pride Lodge . . . nothing.

"A picture wasn't worth any words this time, apparently," Kyle said, resigned. He closed the laptop and decided he was finished with the camera. He needed to be present now, to stay alert and pay close attention to his surroundings and the people in it. Sometimes the camera was a way of hiding, of giving himself to distraction. He would put it in the drawer and let his eyes be the camera from here on in. Whatever he'd been looking for in the photographs he had probably missed because of them. The time had come to watch everything closely and commit what he saw to memory.

Kyle's phone vibrated just then and he picked it up. A text had come from Dylan: "Sid leaving, come up in 10."

Kyle got up from the table and put his camera in the dresser.

"Where are you going?" Danny asked, wishing for once that Kyle had answered Imogene's calls instead, that he'd given in to her needs and not pursued something that would certainly lead to trouble.

"I'm meeting Dylan."

"Stay out of this, Kyle. What's Dylan involvement?"

"Nothing, but he can let me into Teddy's room. Hopefully that's where I'll find what I'm looking for."

Kyle slipped on his shoes and grabbed his jacket. "I'll be back, hopefully soon," he said, and opened the cabin door to leave.

"But you don't know what you're looking for!" Danny said too late, as the door closed. Within a minute of Kyle leaving, Danny's worry got the best of him and he began searching for the business card that Detective Linda Sikorsky had given to everyone she had interviewed. Kyle may think he needs to wait, but Danny feared waiting was precisely the wrong thing to do.

Chapter Twenty-Six

TEDDY'S ROOM

Dylan watched from the empty restaurant window as Sid drove off in their Highlander toward town. No sooner was the car out of sight than Kyle came walking up from the cabins. The two men waved at each other, Dylan looking anxious and forlorn in the window.

Kyle had never been upstairs at the Lodge. There had not been any reason to go there, since he and Danny always stayed in the cabin. When he entered the main room, he saw several people he did not know sitting around chatting and drinking coffee, and there in his recliner perch sat Jeremy Johnson, wearing the same clothes he'd been in the night before. Maybe they were duplicates, like someone who dresses only in black. Maybe it's all Jeremy wore.

"Don't tell me you've been here all this time," Kyle said, closing the outside door behind him.

"No," said Jeremy, "I'm still capable of making it up the stairs. And I wasn't here earlier when you came for lunch."

"You know, I didn't notice."

"But I noticed you," Jeremy said, winking.

Kyle was struck again by how enigmatic Jeremy was: the guest who'd been coming the longest, whose presence everyone was aware of, but who blended in so well he might be said to be invisible; and he clearly enjoyed his status as a fly on the wall. Kyle knew there couldn't be much that went unnoticed by the old sentinel.

"Speaking of upstairs," Kyle said, nodding at the staircase. "I've never been up there and thought, why not take a look."

"I'm sure Dylan can show you around," Jeremy said, winking again before turning and reaching for his cup of tea, the string dangling over the side.

Kyle suddenly had the idea that Jeremy thought he was having some kind of affair with Dylan. It was unnerving enough to have himself so astutely observed, but that wink when he mentioned Dylan, as if something was going on between them, was a step too far. He made a mental note to set Jeremy straight before the day was over. He would not have anyone, however imaginative, thinking he was cheating on Danny. That was untrue, unfair, and just the kind of innuendo that could spread through Pride Lodge like a brushfire.

He turned then and headed for the stairs, leaving the others to their lively conversation and old Jeremy to his fantasies.

Bo saw him coming up the stairs just as she was about to head out and she quickly backtracked into her room, closing the door until only an inch was open, just enough for her to peer through. She didn't need to know that Kyle had never been upstairs to know something was different. The old man in the chair wasn't the only one skilled at watching, and if there was one thing Bo could spot in human behavior, it was the clandestine. It was the way he climbed the stairs, as if he didn't want to make any noise, didn't want anyone to see him. And then easing his way down the hall, glancing at each door, still moving carefully so he would not alert anyone to his presence. Only a man up to something acted this way. It wasn't even conscious, she knew, but the body's way of accommodating a guilty mind, a mind that feared it might be caught. And when she thought that, she, too, wondered if Kyle Callahan was meeting someone up here, someone with whom he was being unfaithful. Or maybe faith had nothing to do with it. Maybe Kyle and Danny had an arrangement. Bo knew such relationships existed. "Open marriages," they were called. But if that was the case, why the stealth?

And then the door to room 208 opened and Dylan waved at Kyle, equally careful to be quick and quiet. (Her great luck had been to get a room so close, having never been here before, but finding the room assignment exceedingly favorable to her plans.) Her first thought was that this was the man Kyle was having his affair with, but when she saw Dylan hurry Kyle into the dead man's room, glance back out into the hallway to make sure no one had seen, and close the door, she suddenly had a different thought, an uncomfortable suspicion: what if this wasn't about sex at all, but about looking for something with Sid gone? She, too, had watched him drive away, and not more than ten minutes later Kyle Callahan came skulking up the stairs. If the two men were meeting for lust, they could have used any empty room, or met somewhere on the grounds away from prying eyes. It would be macabre in the extreme to meet in a dead man's room for any reason other than to search it. (She knew room 208 was Teddy Pembroke's room because the police had gone through it, but not sealed it off; they were probably looking for a suicide note, just in case Pembroke had decided to end his life in grand fashion by flinging himself to the bottom of an empty swimming pool, martini glass in hand.)

Once Kyle was in the room and the door closed, Bo quietly slipped out, made sure the door was locked, and headed downstairs. Things may be moving more quickly than she'd wanted.

Dylan thought he saw the door to Bo Sweetzer's room opened a crack, then close as Kyle walked by. He gave it only a moment's thought, his mind on more important things, and quietly welcomed Kyle into Teddy's room.

Kyle was taken aback at the thought of anyone living in a single room. He and Danny had always taken Cabin 6 and he never stopped to wonder how small a room seemed without a bathroom. There was only a bed, a dresser, a flat screen TV mounted on a wall, a makeshift kitchen Teddy had set up on a bookcase, with a hotplate, some dishes and cups, and essential items for making coffee. He had eaten all his meals in the restaurant or in town, and he didn't seem to own many clothes. The small closet wasn't even full.

Kyle was able to get the complete tour by simply standing in the middle of the room and turning around.

"Did he have a computer?" he asked. It was unusual these days for someone not to at least have a cheap laptop or a low-end tablet, and he'd emailed Teddy enough times to know he had access to one.

"Teddy wasn't very computer literate," Dylan said. He had slumped down onto the corner of Teddy's bed, his shoulders hunched, clearly not wanting to be in the room. "He would use the guest laptop if he needed to go online. Sometimes he would use ours."

Yes, Kyle thought, he used yours and it got him killed.

"I don't know what you're expecting to find," Dylan said. "Teddy was a simple man in most ways. You can see he didn't own much."

Well, of course not, Kyle thought, there's no place to put anything!

"I just want to look around. You're right, there's probably nothing here, but humor me a moment."

And then he saw it: the "Big Book" of Alcoholics Anonymous. On the shelf underneath the coffee pot and hotplate. It was their bible of sorts, the text they used to turn their lives around. Kyle only knew what he'd learned about "the program", as it was called by people in it, from friends and acquaintances he had known. He had never even held their book, and when he took it from Teddy's shelf he had the odd sensation he was holding some sort of holy manuscript.

He started slipping slowly through the pages and saw that Teddy had underlined dozens of passages. As he looked at the book he was more convinced than ever that Teddy was sober when he died, that he had changed his life and would never knowingly end it with the appearance of a drunkard's death. And then, toward the back, he came upon Page 417, so often quoted by Teddy Pembroke. Acceptance. It was a passage on this page that Teddy repeated over and over, like a nun reciting her rosary. Kyle opened the pages and there, slipped between them, was a piece of paper. He took it out and opened it: an email.

"What's that?" Dylan asked, getting up from the bed. He walked over, staring at the sheaf of paper as Kyle read it over:

From: "Sam Tatum" <s.tatum@zipmail.com:>
To: "Sid_Stanhope323@inboxx.com>
Wednesday, September 12

Sid – Lucky we even stayed in touch, surprised you would, but maybe not. Maybe I was the canary in the mine for you. Frank was for me, that's for damn sure. I can't say God rest his soul. That's a man who's soul won't ever rest and shouldn't. Stone cold killer, Frank was, and look at what it cost us. Someone's coming, I don't know who. Frank was killed in Detroit and I know it wasn't random, they came for him. I only know because he owed me money and some lawyer called to say he was paying me back, from the grave. Landlord found him with a bullet in the head and an empty watch box. Watch box, think about it. Two months later and still no suspects. It's only a matter of time for you and me, you should know, that's why I wrote. You gotta keep a look out, check in sometimes, make sure I'm still alive. Kidding. Not really. I'm not counting on being around too much longer. I'm too old and tired to run. I think instead I'll just get some more nose candy and a pretty young man to share it with. Yes, I haven't changed. No, I don't care what anyone thinks. This is some serious shit. I thought we'd made it, but some things you just can't escape. – Sam

"The 23rd is when we met," Dylan said, sounding fanciful.

"What?"

"His email name, Sid Stanhope323. Our anniversary is March 23rd. That's sweet."

Kyle thought it was an odd time to be sentimental. He'd just read an email that implicated Sid in something terrible, something that would make someone want to kill three men, and he was sure he knew what it was.

"Where does Sid come from?" Kyle asked.

Dylan looked at him as if it was the strangest question he'd ever been asked. "What do you mean?"

"When you met him, where did he say he was from?"

"Jersey, always. He was born in Elizabeth and grew up in Newark. His family moved to Atlantic City when he was in high school. What difference does it make?"

"None, for now," Kyle said. "I need to take this, or a copy."

"Take it," Dylan said, exasperated. "I wish I'd never seen it. This is a horrible situation, Kyle. Something's going on, something awful, and Sid's involved. The guy in the email said as much."

The guy in the email may well be dead, Kyle thought, not saying it. If his warning was right, someone had killed one of the three already, and since they'd now moved on to Sid, it seemed likely that Sam Tatum's next communication, if there was any, would be from beyond the grave.

Dylan's mood had darkened still further and he spoke softly, almost in a whisper. "Do you think this has anything to do with the money?"

"What money?" Kyle asked, folding the email and slipping it into his shirt pocket.

"The money for the Lodge!" Dylan said sharply, as if Kyle had not been paying attention when he should.

"I don't know what the connection is, or if there even is one. I'm going to give this to Detective Sikorksy and see what she makes of it. Whoever's in on this game isn't going to stop now, and if they've killed several times already, they're dangerous indeed."

"'They,'" Dylan said. "You make it sound like there's more than one."

"If you mean more than one killer, I'm afraid so."

Dylan visibly shivered, rubbing his hands on his upper arms as if a sudden chill had slipped into the room. "What do I do?"

"Wait, just a little while longer," Kyle said. "I think by tonight we'll have all the answers we need."

"None of them answers we want," Dylan said sadly. "None of them."

Kyle nodded, aware that as the threads came together it would weave a very different life from the one Dylan had been living, had dreamed himself living. Hopefully no more lives would be lost, but everything, for Dylan and the Lodge, would be changed.

Chapter Twenty-Seven

CABIN 6

yle had not stopped pacing since returning from Teddy's room two hours earlier. He had shown Danny the email, providing the evidence he had insisted he needed to take to Detective Sikorsky. On learning that Danny had already reached her and that she was coming that evening, he had decided not to add fuel to the fire for now. He would wait patiently and give her the email when he saw her. After that, he expected things to move rapidly.

"Why don't you call Imogene back?" Danny said, having watching Kyle try to sit still and repeatedly fail. It was the last thing he thought he would ever suggest, but he wanted something to distract Kyle from the escalating events at the Lodge. "It'll take your mind off this."

"I don't want to take my mind off this. Focus, Danny, it's time for me to focus."

"Wearing a hole in the carpet is not focusing. She's going to start calling the hospitals, you know."

"Who?" Kyle said, turning on his heel toward Danny. "The detective? Whatever for?"

"Noooo! Imogene. You never ignore her completely like this, unless we're in the middle of the ocean and there's no cell phone reception. I know you sneak texts to her when you think I'm not looking, it's okay."

Kyle sighed and sat at the table, channeling his restless energy into his shaking foot. "She doesn't even know where we are. I mean she does and she doesn't. Manhattan is her universe, get her outside the City and she doesn't know east from south. All she knows is we're in the countryside somewhere, which to her is the entire continent, with the possible exceptions of Los Angeles and Chicago."

Kyle took the email from Teddy's room out of his shirt pocket, flattened it on the table and read it over again.

"It hasn't changed since the last time you read it," Danny said. He was doing his best not to get caught up in Kyle's anxiety. "You act like it's going to disintegrate if you don't keep handling it."

Kyle didn't respond for a moment, choosing to lose himself in thought instead. "It seemed a little easy, " he said.

"What did?"

"Finding this! I can't be the only one Teddy was always quoting that passage from the AA book to. It was his mantra, 'Page 417, 'Acceptance is the answer to all of my problems today.' He'd repeat it two or three times in a conversation. It's almost as if someone wanted me to find it."

"He did!" Danny said, exasperated. "Teddy wanted you to find it! He was afraid something might happen to him."

Kyle wasn't fully convinced and let his imagination take over, trying to make connections of events that seemed random. Teddy's death, Happy's body found in the creek. Sid was a killer, or at least a bystander to murder. He'd been there in the Lapinsky home when it happened. And so had Bo Sweetzer, then young Emily. And now the collision course they'd been on was coming to a head.

"Imogene will survive," Kyle said absently, trying again to regain his composure, and the mention of his boss gave him a most unexpected idea. "Maybe she can turn it into something for Tokyo Pulse."

"Oh, great," Danny said. "Never miss an opportunity when there's news to be made. She really has you trained."

"That's not what I mean. But there's a story here. They're looking to beef up their general news and she wants off the finance beat, she doesn't have the head for it."

"She has a head?!" Danny said, trying to bring a little levity to the situation.

Kyle frowned. "She's a very good reporter, Danny. It's not that she can't do this job, it's just that it bores here. You have to admit finance is not very sexy. She might be able to take a story about murder at a country resort and get some attention."

"Don't forget the 'gay' part. Pretty soon we'll be completely assimilated and lose the curiosity factor, better hurry."

Kyle waved him off, not willing to get further into it. It was not that he disrespected his friend Teddy, or the Lapinksy family, or anyone else. But he was a realist as well. For one thing, they were all dead and wouldn't care, and for another, someone should tell their story, it was a hell of a feature, and not some talking head from Philly6, either. The story was going to be reported regardless of how Kyle or Danny or anyone else felt about it. It might as well be Imogene who broke it.

"I'm going to call her back," Kyle said, and he got his phone from the dresser. He dialed Imogene, glancing at his watch as he did: 5:30 p.m. They would need to leave soon for dinner and the party.

"Imogene, it's Kyle," he said into her voicemail as he headed into the bathroom to get ready. "There's a story here you might be interested in. Not Manhattan-local obviously, we're in Pennsylvania, but a seriously meaty story with history and cold cases and more angles than you could shake a microphone at. Maybe Lenny-san would go for it." He was referring to her boss, Leonard Baumstein, who ran the small newsroom and reported up to his boss in Japan. "Call me when you can."

"I don't know about you, Kyle," Danny said from the living room.

"I don't always know about me, either," Kyle said, "but I'm in the land of the living and Teddy's dead. He's not coming back, he wouldn't care who told the story. Hell, he would've been the first to tell me to call her anyway. He always liked attention, so why not give him that?"

Kyle closed the bathroom door before Danny could say anything else. Danny shook his head, reached for the remote and un-muted the television just in time for the local news. He had the uneasy feeling they would all be part of it the next time he turned it on.

Chapter Twenty-Eight

ROOM 202

Bo sat on the bed staring across at the wall. It felt to her almost like a trance state; she would know because she had been in this state before, just before killing Frank Grandy and Sam Tatum. A calm overtook her, and a sadness, too. Especially this night. It brought a finality the others did not. She had to admit that once she'd found Grandy and set off on her mission there was a sense of anticipation, of taking the next step, but after tonight there would be no more steps. Or, rather, she would be stepping finally into oblivion.

She would be fooling herself to think they wouldn't connect her to this murder, and then the others. For all she knew, Linda Sikorksy had already been following her leads and instincts and may be closer to the truth than Bo could guess. She would be driving off from Pride Lodge, going west somewhere, maybe Chicago, where she would stop and plan, stop and re-arrange. She would never see St. Paul again.

She took her father's gun from the velvet cloth she kept it wrapped in and held it in her lap. It felt heavier tonight. It weighed on her in a way it hadn't before. The last time she used in, in Frank Grandy's apartment in Detroit, it had seemed almost weightless, an extension of her hand. She had felt exhilarated, so thrilled to be able at last to silence the cries of he' parents' ghosts that she nearly levitated, or at least it felt that way. She had no remorse when she shot Grandy; certainly no more than he had had when he shot first her father, then her mother. Bang, bang. Just like that. Why hadn't she cried out from the closet? Was it fear, or was there an instantaneous determination to survive this, and to survive it for vengeance? Could a ten year old girl in the moment of her life's greatest crisis really be that calculating?

Yes, she thought. Yes, I was. Maybe I'm just cold inside and always have been. Maybe when I saw my father shot I knew then and there I would shoot back someday. Shoot back, or stab back, or strangle back, but the score would be settled, and yes, I knew even then.

She felt foolish in her cat costume. She was not a cat by nature. A serpent, perhaps, patient and deadly, but not a cat. That was part of her thinking, she knew, to obfuscate who she was and why she was here. It distorted the picture anyone might form of her, and distortions served her purpose. Cats did not shoot people, although they did pounce, and the thought of it made her smile. She reached up with her free hand and touched her face, so peculiar did the smile feel. Her smile had never been genuine since the day her parents died. It was a mask, a device, and suddenly the falseness of it startled even her.

She rose slowly, slipping the gun beneath the waistband of her costume. She would go to the party, smile and be a Halloween cat for a time, and she would wait. Once the opportunity came, and it would, she would lure Sid away from the crowd having its party, and she would put an end to him and to it, this lifelong ache and obsession. Within minutes after that, she would be gone. As for luring him, that might not be the right word. Challenge would be more accurate, since he knew who she was. He'd made that clear, and he would be looking for a chance of his own. Who struck first would decide the matter, and she had no doubt about who that would be.

Chapter Twenty-Nine

THE MASTER SUITE

Sid knew he should leave now. Maybe his instincts were too rusty after all these years; he hadn't had to act this quickly since the day he fled Los Angeles. And maybe it was sentiment, hesitation from loving the life he had with Dylan. A soft life, despite the demands of running a resort. A life of love and coffee in the mornings and the absolute quiet of the Pennsylvania countryside. He would never see it again, and he wanted to make as slow an exit as he could, providing it did not ensnare him.

Dylan was already downstairs at the party. He had been too nervous to linger in the Suite. He loved this life, too, but he worried much more about the details and the requirements than Sid did. Dylan was a fretter. He'd gone to the basement an hour before anyone else would arrive, determined to have every chair in place, every balloon and paper ghost. The good thing about his being so distracted was that Sid would be able to leave quickly, quietly and unnoticed. He just wanted one more look around, one more deep breath of air he would not breathe again.

He was taking only a suitcase with him. There was no need for more. He had no idea how to go about changing his identity if it came to that. He knew he could learn much from Bo Sweetzer, but she was the last person he ever wanted to see again. She had destroyed his life and it wasn't fair.

He had not pulled the trigger. He hadn't even taken anything from the house! Yet she had targeted him and Sam for revenge, as well as the only man who really deserved it. Could he blame her? Yes, he could. He could blame her for saving her rage all these years and aiming it at an old man who had never meant her harm. Her obsession was costing him everything.

There was no plan A, let alone a plan B. His only plan was to get in his car and drive to New York City, or Queens or the Bronx. Somewhere he could melt into the urban landscape and make a plan. He'd have to get rid of the car. Maybe not get another one, cars were too easy to find. In a big city like New York or Boston he could live out his life never driving again. Would he need to change his name? How, exactly, does someone do that?

He was thinking it all through, trying to let it gel into definite, clear actions he could take, when a knock came at the door.

Odd, Sid thought. No one ever came to the Suite. Dylan would just walk in, of course. He sighed, annoyed that one of the guests would take the liberty of bringing some minor problem to his attention here, where he lived, and here was considered off-limits, even if there was no official policy about that. There were boundaries to keep, and someone was crossing them.

Sid left the small suitcase on the bed and went to answer the door. Whoever it was, with whatever needless complaint they had, could be dispatched quickly enough and he could get on with the sad task of saying goodbye without uttering a word.

Chapter Thirty

UNHAPPY HALLOWEEN

After falling off some the last few years that Pucky and Stu owned Pride Lodge, the Halloween party was back to its all time highs. Fifty-six guests, not including staff, and another seventy-five locals that Dylan had counted, all packed into the basement bars that had been turned into one large frightfest. No detail had been spared that day as every hand on deck spun cobwebs, hung spiders and placed cackling witches and howling skulls along the bar and table tops. DJ Slam, a college kid from Princeton, had driven in to make $500 for the night and keep the crowd on its feet.

The space was dark, and as Kyle and Danny ordered drinks at one of the corner tables in Clyde's, Kyle had trouble telling the guests from the locals, and one person from another. He thought he saw Maggie dressed as a firefly, taking pictures on her smartphone, and Eileen not far from her as a mummy ordering beer at the bar.

"What do you think is going to become of the place?" Danny asked, having to raise his voice over a Lady GaGa song being played too loud for his tastes. Danny had never liked loud music, or any music when he was talking, and would even turn the radio news off in the car when they were having a conversation. It all became noise to him, especially when it was competing with him.

"Dylan's still here," Kyle said, sipping his margarita while continuing to scan the crowd.

"You think he'll still want to be here if Sid . . ."

"Go ahead, say it. If Sid goes to prison. I can't imagine Dylan leaving under any circumstances."

"What if the bank takes the property?"

Kyle had thought about that. If Dylan was right and Sid embezzled the money to buy Pride Lodge, the bank was going to want its money back. Kyle had no idea what the laws were about something like that, but he imagined they favored the bank.

"Maybe they'll come to some arrangement. I can't imagine the bank wants an old, sprawling gay lodge on its hands, and selling it's a pain. They'd take a loss, I'm sure. And anyway, it's all conjecture. Wait and see."

Danny was first to spot Detective Sikorsky coming through the door. She'd taken the easy way out, costume-wise, and was wearing just a long black wig, witch's hat and cape, the kind of costume a mother would throw together quickly for a child.

"Good thing she's not in the fashion industry," Kyle said as Sikorsky waved and approached the table.

A sudden gasp of recognition went up in the room. Kyle, Danny, and even Linda mid-stride turned to the door that connected Clyde's with the karaoke room and saw none other than Pucky Green standing in the doorway, smiling at everyone. He had forgone a costume, either not wanting to wear one or, more likely, wanting to make sure everybody recognized him. He hadn't been to Pride Lodge in nearly two years, and even though people had speculated all weekend he would come, there was an assumption that he might not. It was a hard place for Pucky to be, as haunted by his memories and it ever could be by make-believe ghosts and plastic goblins.

"Who's that?" Sikorsky asked, sliding into a seat across from Danny.

"That's Pucky Green," Danny said. "The original owner of Pride Lodge, the visionary."

"Ah, yes," she said. She was aware of the Lodge's history, having looked into it quickly the last thirty-six hours. "He moved to Key West after his partner died. On the steps, no less."

The three of them were silent a moment, watching partygoers make their way to Pucky for a hug or a handshake, several of them trying to get him to sit with them. He seemed to prefer staying near the door, holding court for a time, and deserving to. If Pride Lodge truly belonged to anyone, it was Pucky.

"So," the detective said, turning back in her seat, "what's this evidence you have for me?"

Kyle reached into his jacket pocket for the email. He wasn't sure it constituted evidence, or of what: that Sid had a dark past, that he was possibly involved in a crime? That Bo Sweetzer was connected, and that somehow it had all come together and caused the death of Teddy, and perhaps Happy? Were there others?

"He put it where I would find it," Kyle said, handing the email to her. "In his AA book. He was always quoting a page, and sure enough . . ."

"Convenient," she said, unfolding the email.

"I told you," Kyle said.

"Shh." Danny hushed him as Sikorsky read over the message.

Linda Sikorsky folded the email back up and put it in her blouse pocket. "This isn't much, you know. And anyone could have written it."

"But anyone didn't," Kyle said. It came from that man, Tatum. He's dead, I read about it before dinner. An ice pick in the back of his head."

"And you think Bo Sweetzer had something to do with that?" She felt herself blushing and was glad for the darkness of the bar. She had gone out with Sweetzer, not a date by any stretch, but still a revealing of herself. With a murderer? A criminal? She felt her stomach dropping.

"She's not Bo Sweetzer," Kyle said. "At least she wasn't always. She was Emily Lapinsky, I'm sure of it." And to Danny, "I should have brought that photograph, I could've used the Lodge printer. The resemblance is obvious."

"The timing's not right," Sikorsky said, her mind starting to work out the puzzle. "She was here the night before Teddy Pembroke's death, but what about Happy? And why would she kill Pembroke in the first place?"

"She wouldn't," Danny said. "That's the point."

"It's Sid," said Kyle. "There are two killers at Pride Lodge. That's where this is taking me."

Austin came up to the table carrying a tray of drinks. He was wearing a Frankenstein costume, complete with bolts in his neck. He looked the way the monster would if he'd been a post-Stonewall punk with blond and purple hair. "Courtesy of Mr. Hern," he said, handing each of the three a special drink the bar had come up with just for this party. "Monster Mashes," Austin explained.

"Of course," Kyle said.

Danny peered around the room, trying to locate Linus Hern and his pocket-sized entourage. "Why would Linus Hern buy us drinks?"

"A truce?"

"More likely slow acting poison."

"Do you want them or not?" Austin asked.

"You can just leave them on the table," Danny said. "And please tell Mr. Hern we appreciate the gesture."

Austin set the drinks down and hurried off.

"He's up to something," Danny said, taking the drink and sniffing it. "No faint smell of almonds. Cyanide's out."

"You two really don't like each other, do you?" Sikorsky said.

"It's a hate-hate relationship," Kyle said. "And a long story. I'd even say they respect each other, the way a cobra respects a mongoose."

"Please tell me I'm the mongoose," Danny said.

Pucky had been making his way around the room, choosing not to sit anywhere. He was enjoying the attention, the glad-handing and congratulations, although he wasn't sure why anyone would congratulate him. For still being alive? For surviving Stu's death? He had arrived that evening and the "welcome backs" had not stopped since. He walked up to the trio's table just as Danny was hoping to be the mongoose.

"I see you more as a cobra," Pucky said to Danny, extending his hand. "Patient and wise."

Danny would have none of the hand shaking and quickly stood instead, putting his arms around the old man. "You're looking great," he said.

Pucky was dressed like someone who lived in Key West, with lime green pants, a beige sweater and what looked like dock shoes, the kind you see people wearing on a cruise ship. Or a beach.

"I've gained a few," Pucky said. He turned to hug Kyle, who'd also stood, as had the detective. It just seemed the right thing to do, paying deference to a Pride Lodge legend.

"Linda Sikorsky," she said, extending her hand. Pucky took it in both of his and welcomed her to the Lodge, just as he would have when he ran it.

"Sit, sit," Danny said, and to their surprise Pucky agreed. Apparently he was weary of walking slowly around the room hugging and shaking, shaking and hugging.

"Ah," Pucky said, seeing the drinks. "You're enjoying the Monster Mashes. I have no idea what's in them. Creme de Menthe from the look of it."

"Please," Danny said, "have mine."

Pucky thought about it a moment, then agreed, taking the green drink and sipping. He made a face as if to say the Monster Mash was monstrous, and put the drink back on the table.

The conversation veered away then from emails, murders and criminals. Pucky told them about his life in Key West, and how his only regret is that he didn't go there more often with Stu. He talked about life on the island and his neighbors, and the near-perfect climate. Kyle could tell by the tone of his voice and the sadness that kept coming into his eyes that life in the Keys, while no doubt as enjoyable as Pucky said it was, was still life without Stu and that hole would never be filled.

"You could always come back here," Danny said. "Maybe in the summers."

"No," Pucky said. "My time has passed here. I'm sure they'd have me, and maybe even put me to work! But we have to let go eventually. Of everything, and everyone."

"The timing was certainly perfect," Kyle said. "You wanted to go, and Sid and Dylan were there. I can't imagine what would have happened to this place if Sid hadn't had the money."

Pucky looked at him. "Sid?" he said. "Oh, Sid didn't have the money. Jeremy did."

Kyle stared at him. "Jeremy?" he said. "Old Jeremy who sits in the chair for hours and stays up till two in the morning?"

"What other Jeremy is there? He lent them the money, I know that for a fact."

The significance of this information was lost on Danny and Detective Sikorsky. They both waited for Kyle to speak, not sure where he was going with this.

"Pucky, it's great to see you again," Kyle said, as he stood up quickly from the table. "You'll have to excuse us."

Kyle turned to Sikorsky. "We've been played," he said. "We need to go upstairs, now. Have you seen Sid or Dylan?"

"Come to think of it, no" she said.

"Now," Kyle said again, and he lead the way as the three of them hurried out of the bar.

"Where are we going?" Danny asked as they headed up the stairs.

"To stop a murder," Kyle replied, taking the stairs two at a time now. "I hope."

Chapter Thirty-One

AND THE WINNER IS . . .

Dylan was standing in the doorway to the Suite, his face frozen in shock. He was babbling under his breath as Kyle, Danny and Detective Sikorsky hurried down the hallway toward him.

"She killed him," he said, holding out his bloody hands. "She killed Sid."

Sikorsky eased Dylan to the side as the three of them filed into the living room. The scene was horrific. Sid was at his desk, the X-Acto knife from the pumpkin carving sticking grotesquely from his throat. And there, next to his computer keyboard, was the Cinderella pumpkin Bo Sweetzer had carved.

"I tried to save him," Dylan said, still dazed. "I should have taken the knife out . . . I didn't know . . . why would she do that?"

Linda Sikorsky had been to her share of murder scenes, more than one might guess for a place like New Hope, but this one ranked among the worst. Sid Stanhope was now a corpse in a chair, with a considerable amount of his blood drained from his neck onto his shirt, his pants, his shoes, the floor. No one, she knew, could lose that much blood and survive. The knife had been buried fully half its length into his neck. She did not immediately reach for her phone; calling the paramedics now was pointless.

Sid was as dead as Sam Tatum had been when a mother and daughter came upon his lifeless body.

"What am I going to do?" Dylan sobbed. He buried his face in his hands.

"You can start by telling the truth," Kyle said. There was no compassion in his voice.

Everyone turned to Kyle, startled by what he'd said.

"My husband's dead!" Dylan shrieked. "That maniac killed him!"

"I doubt she would make it so obvious after killing two other men quite efficiently," Kyle said coldly, staring at Dylan. "This is more the work of someone local. Someone very close to Sid. About six feet away, as a matter of fact."

Dylan suddenly seemed not quite so shocked, not quite so shaken by the death of his partner, as he began to quickly appraise the situation. Kyle could see it in his eyes, the instant calculation.

"The police are already here," Dylan said, and to Linda, "Arrest her! She can't be far, you have to find her! Do something!"

Detective Linda Sikorsky thought she'd seen it all, but this was rattling her. The only clear victim in the room was dead in a chair. But who was the killer? Who should she be arresting?

Kyle glanced out the window then and saw a pair of taillights disappearing down the road. "I think she's gone by now," he said, turning back to them. "Probably hours ago."

"But Sid stole the money," Dylan cried, desperate to cast the blame on anyone but himself. "And he did something terrible, years ago, it was in that email. Someone wanted him dead."

"They did indeed," Kyle said. "There was no embezzlement. Sid was a criminal, there's no doubt about that, but he didn't steal a dime from the bank. The money came from old Jeremy. Dylan only wanted us to think Sid was a thief."

"Why in hell would I want that?" Dylan demanded, now a very different man from the one who'd been standing in the doorway when they came up the stairs.

"Because it's all yours now," Kyle replied. "Or it would have been, had Pucky not shown up. Not a bad plan, Dylan. Not a flawless one, but you could have gotten away with it. Sid gone, the Lodge and inheritance, whatever there was, yours free and clear with just a sizable loan to repay. Bo Sweetzer – or should I say Emily Lapinsky – blamed for the murders. Who would believe her if she denied it? And Jeremy bankrolling the whole thing, unaware of what you've done. He is unaware, isn't he? I just can't see him as a partner in crime."

"You're out of your mind. She killed him. I have no idea why she was careless. For the same reason she brought the pumpkin, so everyone would know it was her!"

"You mean so everyone would *think* it was her."

Linda Sikosrky stepped toward Dylan. "You're under arrest, Mr. Tremblay."

"Arrest? Me?! For what?!" Dylan shouted.

"For finishing the job Bo Sweetzer started," Kyle said. "For Teddy, for poor Happy, just a kid who couldn't keep his mouth shut. Is that what happened, he told you what Teddy told him, what Teddy found out, and the wheels were set in motion? You're a monster, Dylan. And as bad a man as Sid was, I wish he'd lived to know it."

Dylan thought about running, dashing out of the room and through the Lodge front door, but he knew there was nowhere to go. How far could he get? Everything he owned was here. Better to try and talk his way out of this later. What proof was there? He'd been careful every step of the way. He would find a way out of this, he believed that, he had to believe it. In the meanwhile it was time to be silent, to give them nothing that could and would be used against him, and to think.

Detective Sikorsky finally pulled out her phone and started making calls. The coroner's office for a dead man, back up to help her get Dylan Tremblay to the station house. It was going to be a very long night.

Chapter Thirty-Two

IN THE REARVIEW MIRROR

She'd had the chance to do it, then and there, and yet she had refrained. Hesitated. Was it the influence of her evening with the woman she would never see again, the beguiling detective from New Hope? Or had vengeance run long enough through her veins?

She'd left her room and headed downstairs when she was suddenly, strangely, compelled to see this man face-to-face again. She had thought her reasoning was to tell him the end was near. So near, in fact, it was *here*, right then and there, and she would shoot him in his doorway. But when he had answered her knock – her hand sliding to her waist where the gun could be slipped out quickly – she had stopped hating, just for an instant, just long enough for the two of them to stare silently at one another.

Finally, she said to the man she had been waiting thirty years to kill, "Why did you do that to me?"

Sid thought a long moment, even as he expected to die any second, and said, "You weren't supposed to be there."

"Well," Bo said to him, "I was. And now, I'm here. I'll be downstairs, waiting. I know you'll come. There's no way around this. You know that as well as I do."

Sid nodded. She was right. He could run, but she would find him. She was that determined. He had closed the door then and gone back to his desk to sit and think. Maybe the best thing to do was call the police, to give himself up, to be done with it once and for all. He was trying to decide his course of action when the door opened and Dylan came in, carrying a pumpkin.

Bo knew they would probably catch up with her eventually. When she saw the three of them rush out of the bar – Kyle, Danny and the detective – she knew it was time to go. At first she'd thought Sid might have killed himself, but whatever had happened, an alarm had been sounded and her plans had changed in the instant. She had been at this long enough to know something big had happened, and the time for an escape was now or never.

They had not seen her. She had been alone in the crowd, watching and waiting. She had planned to give Sid another hour to show up, then she would go looking for him. He would be waiting, too, she knew that. Waiting to die, or to kill her instead. And now, just like that, everything had changed.

She drove away from Pride Lodge with nothing but her purse and a gun that would soon be rusting at the bottom of the Delaware River. She could not have gone back to her room, and she knew she was leaving everything behind her, including Bo Sweetzer. She'd glanced in the rearview mirror as she drove down the hill, wondering what name she would take next, when she swore she saw Kyle Callahan in an upstairs window. But of course he had no way of knowing it was her car, if he'd seen it at all.

She drove carefully along to the highway, thought of making a left turn, then made a right instead, and disappeared into the night.

Chapter Thirty-Three

CHECK OUT TIME IS 11:00 A.M.

Seventeen messages. That's how many times Imogene had tried to reach Kyle, once he added up voicemail, texts and two tweets. He'd tried to tell her that, while he had a Twitter account for his photoblog feed that would send out new posts with photos when he put them up, he never actually tweeted. Not with his phone, not with his thumbs, not in any way. So trying to reach him @AsKyleSeesIt was like people who tried to communicate with him through Facebook messages. He seldom ever looked to see what was there.

It didn't matter anyway. He had seen Imogene's car drive past ten minutes earlier. There weren't many like it, a vintage, pink 1968 Mustang that only Imogene Landis would be seen driving. He knew she was at the Lodge now, already asking questions, and he regretted having called her in the first place. Danny was right: it was unseemly, and it appeared, however much Kyle told himself the appearance was deceiving, to be taking advantage of a particularly bad situation. Three people were dead, not counting the men in Los Angeles and Detroit. Having a mouthy livewire like

Imogene show up with a microphone, reporter's notebook and handlheld HD camera made it all seem so . . . *DeathWatchNewHope.*

"You can't hide forever," Danny said, putting the last of his clothes in his suitcase. "She's at the desk now, pestering poor Ricki for details. Ricki and anyone else unlucky enough to show up this early."

"I never should have called her," Kyle said. He was packing up his camera, wondering if he'd taken any good pictures at all, then feeling guilty for caring.

"It's not so much that you called her, Sweetie," Danny said. "But that you never called her again!"

"We were a little busy," Kyle reminded him. "We spent what, two hours at the police station giving statements? I didn't get to sleep until three a.m. this morning, and that was fitful."

"Murder doesn't care. Hell, we're lucky that's all the time we were there. At least we get to leave! Dylan Tremblay won't be seeing the outside of a jail cell for a very long time."

"Nor should he," Kyle said, with a little too much righteousness.

"Nor should he," Danny agreed.

The two then fell silent as they continued packing for their exit from Pride Lodge. Finally, Danny said, "Do you think they'll find her?"

"It would only be right," Kyle said, not looking at him. He knew it was highly unlikely that the taillights he'd seen from the upstairs window were those of Bo Sweetzer. They hadn't even known she'd fled until later, when the police who came to support Linda Sikorsky found no trace of her except the clothes and pocket watch she'd left in her room. And even if they had been her taillights, what was he supposed to have done? Cried out for someone to chase her? He knew he was simply feeling guilty for having wanted her to get away

"She's a murderer, after all," Kyle said, closing his suitcase. "It would only be right."

When they got to the check out desk Kyle glanced around nervously and asked Ricki in a hushed voice, "Where's Imogene?"

"You mean Genie? The reporter lady?"

Ricki was unusually alert and seemed more than a little excited. Kyle knew it meant he must have already been interviewed, however quickly. An interview with Imogene meant flattery, a wink if the person she was talking to was a straight man, and letting a desk clerk at a countryside gay resort call her "Genie." That really was the giveaway. No one called Imogene Landis "Genie" and lived to tell about it. Except Ricki. Kyle could see it now, the not-too-sophisticated man who'd never lived in a place with more than a few thousand people in it calling the diminutive newswoman "Genie," the way a waitress in a roadside diner calls everyone "Sweetheart," and Imogene saying, "You can call me Genie, everyone does." Anything for the story.

"Yes, her," Danny interjected.

"Oh, she's out by the pool talking to the twins. They're on set-up today."

"She'll love that," Kyle said. "What murder in the woods is complete without a set of identical twins? But it gives us a chance to get out of here. I'll just say I didn't see her, didn't know she'd come. Give me ten minutes down the road and I'll call."

"As long as you tell her we're just about into the Lincoln Tunnel. No turning around! You know she'll ask."

It was then Kyle realized that the Lodge had gone on, even with Sid dead and Dylan in jail. He and Danny had missed the coroner's van coming to take Sid's body away. They'd missed the other cops helping to handcuff and incarcerate Dylan. They'd wanted to be away from it as quickly as possible and had headed to the police station in their own car as soon as backup for Detective Sikorsky arrived.

"What happened?" Kyle asked quietly.

"Oh, she asked a few questions, took some footage," Ricki said.

Footage, Kyle thought. Of course Ricki would consider a few minutes on a digital video camera footage, as if he were going to see his name in the final credits at an Imax.

"No," he said. "I mean last night, after . . . you know."

"If you mean, did the band play on? Yes, it did. They put yellow tape up outside the Master Suite, but most of the people downstairs never knew what went on. The cops weren't interested in them, and the staff wasn't about to empty the place. It's our best weekend!"

That thought struck Kyle and Danny both. Dancers danced on, drinkers drank on. Halloween weekend at Pride Lodge celebrated and partied unfazed as the lives of the very people who provided it were destroyed.

"I told them to stay the course," a voice said from behind them. "They weren't being greedy, if that's what you're thinking."

Kyle and Danny turned to see Jeremy standing just a few feet away, leaning slightly on a cane in his left hand. He was doing just fine without the walker today. He seemed much sturdier this way, not like the frail old man everyone imagined him to be. Kyle wondered if that had been what he wanted them all to think. He was a cagey sort, an observer and listener, for whatever his purposes.

"Pucky told me you were the silent partner here," Kyle said. "That's how I knew, how the pieces fell together. Dylan wanted me, Sikorsky, everyone, to think Sid had stolen all that money."

"They weren't a happy couple," Jeremy said. "At least not Dylan. Sid, probably, he was older, his options more limited, by time if nothing else. But Dylan wanted his freedom, as long as it came with the property."

"If you knew all this, why didn't you say anything?" Danny asked.

"Say anything about what? I never imagined Dylan Tremblay would kill people to get what he wanted. I thought he'd stick it out, maybe try for something in a divorce. Honestly, I thought he would even just wait it out. Sid was in poor health, he'd probably die at least twenty years before Dylan. The whole thing is conjecture anyway."

"Correction, Jeremy," Kyle said. "Teddy dead at the bottom of the pool is not conjecture. Happy dead in a creek is not conjecture. And Sid dead upstairs with a knife sticking out of his neck is not conjecture."

Jeremy had defended himself as much as he intended to. " I can't help it that my imagination is not as vivid as yours, Kyle," he said with a shrug. "We're going to need new innkeepers here. I don't suppose I could get the two of you . . ."

"Not on your life," Danny said. "Pride Lodge is a great place to visit, and I'm sure we'll be back, but running a resort is the last thing I would ever want."

"True, true," the old man said. "I expect you'll be running Margaret's Passion soon enough. No one lives forever, it's just the way life goes. But have it your way. For now I've got Ricki, the twins, Cowboy Dave, everyone really, except the owners! Oh wait, that's me."

"So the place is yours?" Kyle asked.

"It is now," Jeremy said. "Sid and Dylan made monthly payments to me, with Pride Lodge itself as collateral. If for any reason the loan was not paid off, which I imagine it won't be now, the Lodge becomes mine. Had I died first that wouldn't be the case. Apparently Dylan didn't think of everything or I'd be the one dead at the bottom of a pool. I'm not the old fool people take me for, you know."

Kyle smiled at him. "I never thought you were. But that's what you want people to think. Camouflage. Pretty impressive, too. It probably saved your life."

Jeremy stuck out his right hand. "So, boys, onward and downward."

Kyle and Danny each shook his hand. They knew he hadn't omitted anything out of malice, and that he really had no idea what lengths Dylan was going to to secure a fantasy future for himself.

A sound of laughter floated up from outside. Imogene, "Genie" to Ricki the desk clerk, was working her charm. And she was charming, to anyone who didn't know her as more than an acquaintance or a brief encounter. To her loyal assistant Kyle Callahan she was a terror, but a lovable terror. He was in no mood to have that love tested this morning.

"Quickly," Kyle said to Ricki. "Just the bill. We have appointments with destiny in, oh, about ten minutes."

"Five," Danny said, hurrying them along. "A laugh means she's just about through with them."

"Whoever she is," Jeremy said, "I like the sound of her."

Kyle turned to him. "Yes, I think you would. I think the two of you are going to hit it off very well. You might want to get back in your chair. She's as much a sucker for frail old men as the rest of us."

"Call her," Danny said, signing the credit card slip. "Ten minutes down the road."

"Lincoln Tunnel," Kyle finished. "Got it, now let's go."

They each grabbed the handle of a suitcase and hurried out of the Lodge. They took the steps two at a time as they turned right into the main parking lot. Moments later Danny was pulling out of the drive just as Kyle saw Imogene hurrying down the hillside, waving at them.

"Look the other way!" Kyle said. "Drive! I'll call her back eventually."

"You're going to hear about this for days, Kyle. She may even threaten to replace you."

"Again?!" Kyle said, and the two of them shared a laugh for the first time in nearly two days.

Danny watched Pride Lodge recede in the rearview mirror. "Do you think we'll ever come back?"

"Sure," Kyle said. "It's become an old friend by now, and one thing about old friends is that you want to know what happens to them. We'll be back."

Danny nodded; they would indeed. He turned the first corner and took one last glance in the mirror to see Imogene standing in the road behind them, hands on her hips, wagging her finger at them. She wasn't fooled. And she would never replace Kyle. Love was love.

Next stop on the mystery train . . .

Pride and Perilous
A Kyle Callahan Mystery

Coming Spring, 2013

Kyle Callahan is about to have his first photography exhibit. His partner Danny and his friends have been nudging him a long time to finally show the world the photographs they've all enjoyed. Among those friends is Katherine Pride, owner of the Katherine Pride Gallery in Manhattan's Meatpacking District. Kyle and Danny first met there, and now they're about to enjoy another first . . . if murder doesn't get in the way.

Someone has been killing off artists, a diverse group whose only connection, Kyle realizes, is the very gallery where his first show is about to open. Will it still? Should it? And who is next on the killer's list – Katherine Pride, or Kyle himself?

Be re-introduced to Detective Linda Sikorsky from 'Murder at Pride Lodge,' in the City with her new girlfriend to attend Kyle's show. Here, too, you'll meet Margaret Bowman, 80 year old owner of the restaurant Margaret's Passion and second mother to Danny. Imogene Landis, livewire TV reporter on the far side of her career, making the most of it with assistant Kyle at her side. And of course the odious Linus Hern, up close and personal in his own cutthroat environment, clearing a path in front of him with a tongue as sharp as a saber. Come along as they all gather for a second installment of murder and mayhem, in 'Pride and Perilous,' opening Spring, 2013.

CPSIA information can be obtained at www.ICGtesting.com
Printed in the USA
LVOW011520020613

336541LV00015B/573/P

9 781478 220190